BILL COSBY

UNIVERSAL PICTURES PRESENTS A SAH ENTERPRISES, INC. PRODUCTION

A FILM BY SIDNEY POITIER

BILL COSBY

"GHOST DAD"

KIMBERLY RUSSELL DENISE NICHOLAS IAN BANNEN

MUSIC SCORE BY HENRY MANCINI DIRECTOR OF PHOTOGRAPHY ANDREW LASZLO, A.S.C.

EXECUTIVE PRODUCER STAN ROBERTSON

STORY BY BRENT MADDOCK & S.S.WILSON

SCREENPLAY BY CHRIS REESE AND BRENT MADDOCK & S.S.WILSON

PRODUCED BY TERRY NELSON DIRECTED BY SIDNEY POITIER

DOLBY STEREO IN SELECTED THEATRES

A UNIVERSAL PICTURE

A novel by Mel Cebulash
Based on a screenplay by Chris Reese
and Brent Maddock & S. S. Wilson
Story by Brent Maddock & S. S. Wilson

BERKLEY BOOKS, NEW YORK

GHOST DAD

A Berkley Book / published by arrangement with
MCA Publishing Rights, a Division of MCA, Inc.

PRINTING HISTORY
Berkley edition / July 1990
Special Sales edition / August 1990

For information address: MCA Publishing Rights,
a Division of MCA, Inc., 100 University City Plaza,
Universal City, California 91608.

A BERKLEY BOOK ® TM 757,375
Berkley Books are published by The Berkley Publishing Group,
200 Madison Avenue, New York, New York 10016.

PRINTED IN THE UNITED STATES OF AMERICA

GHOST
DAD

CHAPTER 1

"Danny says that I'm a haunt," Amanda Hopper said. "Is that true?"

Diane Hopper smiled affectionately at her pretty baby sister. "Oh, no, Amanda," she told the five-year-old, "but I really can do the laundry without any help. What you should do is go up and get ready for bed. Dad hasn't finished reading 'The Canterville Ghost' to you, has he?"

Amanda nodded, and her eyes sparkled with enthusiasm. Diane understood Amanda's appreciation of the ghost story. When she was Amanda's age, she had enjoyed listening to her father read the funny tale. In her mind's eye she recalled her mother listening and laughing with her. Amanda was never going to have that experience, Diane thought sadly. "What's the matter?" Amanda asked.

"Nothing," Diane replied, feeling slightly embarrassed. "I was just thinking about how much better Dad can read the story now."

"Really?"

"Practice," Diane explained with a smile. "After reading it to me, then to Danny, and now to you, Dad almost knows the story by heart. Now go on. I'll see you before you go to sleep."

Amanda scooted up the stairs, and Diane grinned at the thought of her little sister's "time" with Dad. He had some weird ways of doing things, but she loved him. The sound of the phone interrupted her thoughts. It was Jonelle Davis, her best friend. "I wanted to be first to wish you a happy birthday," she said.

"Tomorrow."

Jonelle laughed. "I know, but if I waited, I wouldn't be the first. What are you doing?"

"The laundry."

"Oh, sorry. I also called to see if you can guess who I saw at the mall this afternoon."

"A guy?"

"Yeah, but a really super, special guy, and he was asking about you."

"Tell me," Diane said anxiously.

"Tony Ricker!"

"Tony Ricker!" Diane repeated, not willing to believe her ears. "What did he say about me?"

"He wanted to know if you were in the mall, and he seemed disappointed when I told him you were at home. He said he hoped he bumped into you sometime."

"That would be a great birthday present. How did he look?"

"Gorgeous," Jonelle reported.

"I know what you mean," Diane replied, "but I have to get off this phone now and throw another load in the dryer. I'll see you in school."

"Bye."

As Diane pulled clothes from the washing machine she amused herself with thoughts of telling her friends she was going with Tony Ricker. Some would be jealous, but her true friends would be happy for her.

While Diane was considering which friends would act like true friends, Amanda was listening intently to her father's presentation of the ghost story. " 'Sometime after the family had retired,' " Elliot Hopper read, " 'they were awakened by a curious noise in the corridor. It sounded like the clank of metal and seemed to be coming nearer every moment.' "

Amanda smiled. Her daddy's scary tone didn't frighten her.

" 'Father got up at once,' " he continued, " 'put on his slippers and opened the door. Right in front of him he saw the ghost. An old man with eyes red as burning coals; long grey hair coils; his garments were oily and ragged, and from his wrists hung heavy manacles and rusty chains. "My dear sir," said Father, "I really must insist on your oiling those chains, and have brought you for that purpose a small bottle of Tammany Rising Sun Lubricator." ' "

Amanda giggled, and almost as though the giggle were expected, there was a momentary pause in Elliot Hopper's performance. Then he read on, " ' "It is said to be completely effective upon one application and there are several testimonials to that effect on the wrapper." ' With these words, Father laid the bottle down on a marble table, and, closing his door, returned to bed."

Picturing the father in the story insulting the ghost, Amanda giggled again. Daddy was funny, like the father in the story. He would act the same way if he came face-to-face with a ghost. Amanda was sure of that. She could see the scene as she listened to more of the story. Then her father's tone changed. "Okay, honey bun," he remarked, "that's enough for tonight. Sorry I had to work late again this weekend. But remember: It's just until Thursday. Now make me louder and hold me up to the door."

As usual Amanda was sorry her special time with Daddy was over. She quickly reached for the tape player on the nightstand and turned up its volume control. Then she faced the player toward the hallway. A second or so later her daddy's voice called, "Good night, Diane!"

By then Diane was down the hall in Danny's room, dropping off his share of the laundry. She heard her father's recorded message, but she wasn't in the mood for it, especially because she knew he probably wasn't through with her. "Don't wait up for me!" his voice commanded.

"I never do," Diane said, shaking her head at the idea of replying to a tape recording.

"I thought you were too grown-up to answer," Danny said, laughing at his sister.

"Very funny," Diane said, "and how do you plan to reply, Mr. Twelve-year-old?"

Their father's taped voice interrupted. "Good night, Danny!"

After hitting the play button on his cassette player and holding it up, Danny smiled at his older sister. "Good night, Dad!" Danny's voice boomed from the player. "I'll see you in the morning. Good talking to you!"

Danny stopped the player and smiled broadly at Diane. In return Diane shook her head in mock disgust. In the meantime Amanda reached for the tape player and lowered the volume. "Okay, Amanda," her Daddy voice said, "now turn out the light and go to sleep. I love you."

"I love you, too, Daddy," Amanda said, reaching for the tape player and switching it off.

A moment later Diane entered the room. "I have to put away your laundry," she said. "I'll tuck you in and shut the light in a minute."

Amanda was sleeping contentedly by the time Diane tucked her in and gently kissed her. "I love you," Diane whispered, and turned out the light.

When Diane finally got ready for bed, she was exhausted. She was glad Sunday was over. Her day of rest was Monday—in school. It had been a little over two years since her mother had died. Diane had pitched in, helping her father keep things going around the house, but lately most of the work had fallen on Diane's shoulders because her father was working hard for a promotion at his job. On Thursday he was supposed to learn if he had made it. Diane couldn't wait.

Diane glanced out her window and saw several lights on in Joan Bankhead's house. Joan had moved next door about six months earlier. She was a writer and worked at home, except when she had to leave the house for research. She was in her thirties, attractive, and single. The lights made Diane wonder if Joan was working. It was late, but according to Joan, she worked when the "creative urge" hit her.

Diane closed her drapes and climbed into bed. She hoped Joan was working—not sitting around waiting for Elliot Hopper to stop there before going home. Diane knew she wasn't being fair. Her father had been seeing Joan for a few months and Diane actually liked her, but she couldn't get used to the idea of her father having a romantic interest in Joan or any other woman.

CHAPTER 2

Elliot Hopper came home late that night and quietly headed for his bedroom. A flickering light coming from Danny's room caught his attention, and he stuck his head into the room, thinking that his son had fallen asleep while watching TV.

"Hi, Dad," Danny said, looking away from the video game he was playing.

"What are you doing?"

"Dad," Danny answered, seeming puzzled, "you've seen this game before. We played it together. Don't you remember?"

"Of course I remember the game, but what are you doing up? You have school tomorrow. You should be sleeping."

Danny turned on a lamp and switched off his video game. "I wanted to ask you a question about school," he said.

"Danny," his father replied indignantly, "you can't tell me you were playing that game just to pass the time until you had a chance to see me."

Smiling and trying to hide it, Danny said, "Well, I do like the game, but I wanted to talk to you about this Trunk of Doom Magic Kit."

He picked up an open magazine and pointed to an ad on the page. "We'll talk about it in the morning, Danny," his father replied, closing the magazine and reaching for the lamp next to his son's bed. "Now go to sleep."

"Okay, Dad," Danny said reluctantly. "I love you."

"Me too," Elliot Hopper said. "I'll see you in the morning."

When the alarm buzzed the next morning, Elliot wished he could roll over and sleep for a few more hours, but he knew he had to be at work on time. He also had to get Diane and the others up and moving. They liked to sleep, especially on Monday mornings.

As soon as the sleepyheads were awake, Elliot showered. He was shaving when Danny stepped into the bathroom doorway and said, "I need to talk to you."

"Go ahead. I told you I would be happy to hear about the video game in the morning."

"No, Dad," Danny said, trying to hide his disappointment, "it's the Trunk of Doom Magic Kit we need to discuss. I showed you it last night in the ad in the magazine."

Just then Diane stepped up and tried to push past Danny. "Can I get in there, please?" she said.

"Stay calm," Danny said, before turning back to his dad. "I need the kit for Wednesday or I can't do the trick."

"And I need to speak to you, Elliot," Diane said as she handed her makeup kit to Danny and started brushing her hair.

"Take a number and get back in line," Danny remarked, covering the makeup kit with his towel as if he intended to do a trick.

"I'm sorry," his father said. "I completely forgot about your magic kit, Danny, but I'll pick one up for you on the way home."

"Pick one up for me? You have to order it. It has to be shipped. It comes from India, or Chicago. I'm not sure about that. It may be Jersey City, but you have to order it."

"The bathroom is all yours," Elliot announced, quickly stepping past Danny and Diane, "but don't fight over it, and I'll make it up to you about the kit after Thursday. I promise."

"Wait a minute," Danny called.

"You chase him and give me a minute here, please?" Diane said.

Danny pulled away his towel. Diane's makeup kit was gone. It had disappeared. "Oh, no!" she roared. "Where is it?"

"I'll tell you later."

"Danny!" Diane screamed, and charged after him.

She was twisting her brother's arm when her father reappeared. "Let go of Danny's arm," he said, "and you give your sister her makeup kit. The next trick you can do is get dressed in two seconds, and you should also get moving, Diane. Your sister and brother need breakfast. I'll see you downstairs."

"They *always* need breakfast," Diane said sarcastically as she snatched her makeup kit from her brother's outstretched hand.

Guided by the fact that his father had just turned and walked off, Danny decided it wasn't a good time to pursue the matter of the magic kit. Moreover he didn't want to miss breakfast.

As usual Amanda was the first family member seated in the kitchen for breakfast. "How do you always get down here so fast?" Danny teasingly asked upon entering the room. "How do you shave so fast?"

"I don't shave," Amanda replied, a puzzled look on her face.

"That was a joke," Danny explained.

"About getting down here so fast?" Amanda asked.

"How did you two get down here so fast?" Diane asked.

"I forgot to shave," Danny joked.

"Do you shave?" Amanda asked.

"He is joking," Diane said. "Your brother Danny is always joking. In fact, he *is* a joke."

"I want some pancakes and waffles," Amanda replied, "and happy birthday, Diane."

Smiling slightly and nodding her head, Diane quickly started to prepare her little sister's breakfast. "Oh, yeah," Danny added, "happy birthday from me too. I wanted to get you something good, except you're the one who always knows what's good for a present for someone in this house. So I decided my present to you would be the honor of not having to go out and shop for a present for me to give to you. How do you like that for a present?"

"I love it, and I must say that you're a very unusual child, Daniel. You're exactly like your father."

"Thank you for noticing."

"Yeah, and I can imagine the kind of excuse he'll have about my birthday."

"Hey," Danny protested, "let's stop teasing each other. I'm sure Dad wouldn't forget your birthday. He said he was going to see you downstairs. You heard him."

"That didn't mean a thing."

"Listen, Diane, I'm sure he wouldn't forget your birthday."

Elliot Hopper was about to bounce down the stairs and join his children in the kitchen when Danny's confident words hit his ears. He *had* forgotten—completely.

"He probably already forgot," Diane said, "and he'll have some story about making it up to me after Thursday. You know what I mean. He thinks the whole world is going to be different after Thursday."

Elliot was frozen with panic. He wanted to run and hide. How could he have forgotten Diane's birthday? Actually he knew how he had forgotten. He had been putting all his time and energy into a possible promotion at work. If it came through, things were certainly going to be different around the house.

Good, Elliot told himself, *but you have to get moving now.* He turned and looked around. There had to be something he could do—to pretend he hadn't forgotten. The pleasant aroma of cereal cooking caught his attention. Time was running out.

CHAPTER 3

Sometimes Diane cooked whatever her sister and brother wanted for breakfast. This wasn't one of those mornings. She didn't feel happy about her birthday, and she definitely didn't feel happy about playing Mother around the house. It was no fun at all. "Here," she said, sliding a bowl of cereal and a glass of juice in front of Amanda, "are your pancakes and waffles."

"They look wonderful," Danny said. "I'll have two eggs, hash browns, a few strips of bacon and . . ."

Without a word Diane slapped a bowl of cereal and a glass of juice on the table in front of Danny. "Or," he continued, "if the hash browns are too much trouble, I'll settle for some cereal and juice."

Danny's luck with breakfast was much better than his father's luck with a birthday present for Diane. He had been forced to settle on a makeshift birthday cake. In truth, it was nothing more than a mountain of shaving cream on top of a flat-topped hat, and it looked it. The burning candle stuck in the shaving cream didn't help.

Smiling as best he could, Elliot started down the stairs and sang, "Happy birthday to you. Happy birthday to you. Happy birthday, dear . . ."

While Elliot cheerfully pretended to have forgotten Diane's name, he also continued his very slow-paced trip down the stairs. His lead foot seemed to be in line with an object several steps below, which would considerably hasten his trip—one of Amanda's roller skates.

"D—" Diane laughingly provided the letter sound to assist her father.

"Doris," he said, pausing to think, and then added, "Donna, Delores."

"Di—" Diane provided the first syllable as her father continued his slow-motion descent.

"Di-nosaur," Elliot sang. "Di-verticulitis."

At that very moment Elliot's song made Diane, Danny, and Amanda laugh out loud. Simultaneously his lead foot settled on Amanda's roller skate, but, almost as if his luck had turned for the better, he stopped. Reaching down and picking up the skate, he said, "Honey, don't leave your skates on the stairs."

"Sorry," Amanda said.

"Okay," Elliot said, picking up speed and moving into the kitchen, "happy birthday, dear Diane, happy birthday to you."

As soon as Elliot could set down the "cake" and the skate, he hugged Diane—long and hard. Feeling happy, though slightly embarrassed, she said, "Elliot, you don't have to get so mushy with me."

"Hey," he responded, "fathers are supposed to do crazy things some of the time. For my ninth birthday my dad dressed up in a bunny suit."

"I wouldn't call that crazy," Danny chimed in.

"He wore it for a week."

"A whole week?" Danny said.

"Well," Elliot explained, "he only meant to wear it for the day, but the zipper got stuck."

"Sounds as if he was our grandpop," Danny remarked.

Diane laughed in agreement, and as she did, her father leaned over and kissed her on the cheek. "I have to run," he said.

Diane's cheerful expression disappeared. "What?" she roared, turning into a tiger. "You tell me you have to run! It's my seventeenth birthday, and you have to run! When Jonelle turned seventeen, she got a convertible. I got shaving cream! Well, you didn't fool me, Dad. You completely forgot my birthday, but you just can't admit it. I guess it wasn't important enough for you to remember, was it? And that's old news to me."

Elliot paused, trying hard to think of a reply. Finally he mumbled, "Oh, yeah. Is that so?"

"Yeah."

"Well, that's where you're wrong," Elliot said weakly, before turning to Amanda and Danny for support. "Your know-it-all big sister really fell for that one, didn't she? Did you notice how I set her up for it?"

Amanda and Danny stared at him in disbelief. The shaving-cream cake hadn't inspired their confidence. "All right, forget I asked." Elliot shrugged and turned his attention back to Diane. "It just so happens I did not forget your birthday. I couldn't forget your seventeenth birthday. In fact, not only did I *not* forget your birthday, but I got you something so incredibly wonderful that even you would have to call it . . . outstanding."

"Doubtful," Diane replied.

Elliot reached into his pocket and pulled out some car keys. "Do these look doubtful?" he said as he dangled the keys in front of Diane.

"What about them?"

"If Thursday goes the way I expect it to go, I think the company will also be getting me a new car. And guess who is going to be the owner of my present car—the one in the driveway?"

"Grumpy?"

"An unfair nickname, but yes, you guessed it."

Diane loved the idea, but she didn't want to appear too anxious, especially because she still had doubts about the offer. "What's the catch?" she asked.

"No catch. It's yours."

"Excellent," Diane replied, reaching for the keys. "I'll drive it today. I only have one class this morning and—"

"Wait! It's yours on Thursday."

"Oh, please?" Diane begged. "I'll drive you to work. I'll do the shopping. I'll pick you up after work. I'll be careful. I'll stay buckled up even when I'm parked."

"No, Diane! I said Thursday!"

Diane stopped reaching for the keys. She felt heartbroken, and her face showed it. She didn't want to wait until Thursday. She wanted to show her friends what she had gotten from her father for her birthday—on her birthday. She turned and started to walk away.

"Don't give me that sheepdog look," Elliot called after her. "It won't work."

Diane didn't answer, but her heart filled with hope. She recognized something in his tone of voice. Elliot was weakening—fast. She continued toward the front door. "Hold it!" he called as Diane reached for the door handle.

"I'm not giving you any look," she said, turning his way. "I'm just hurt. Can't you understand that?"

"Let's just call a truce for now. Okay?"

Diane bit her lip to keep from smiling. She knew the look of surrender when she saw it. "A truce?" she said. "That's fine with me. Now what?"

CHAPTER 4

Elliot glanced at Amanda and Danny. They looked disappointed. "What's the matter?" he asked.

"Nothing," Danny said.

"Is that right, Amanda?"

"Yes, Daddy, but Diane should have a happy birthday."

Amanda's sad expression was more than Elliot could handle. "Here," he said, handing the keys to Diane, "but if you don't drive right on the way to my office, you'll be taking a cab to school. Go on out there. I have to put out the garbage."

"I'll help you, Daddy," Amanda said cheerfully.

"You just helped your sister," Elliot said, smiling at her, "so I guess you should help me now. Danny, you clear the table."

Although Diane had been expecting to get the keys, she wasn't prepared for the thrill of victory. As her father and Amanda went off to get the garbage can, she stepped over to Danny and showed him the keys. "Can you believe he gave them to me?" she asked.

"Would you like me to make them disappear?"

"No!" Diane replied, quickly moving away from him. "Would you walk Amanda to the day-care center today?"

"Sure," Danny said. "Consider it a birthday present."

"Thanks," Diane called, just before stepping outside.

Stepping quickly and triumphantly, Diane headed for the car. "You won't regret this, pal," she called to Elliot.

Busy carrying the garbage can and still smarting from the agony of defeat, he could only generate a weak smile. Once he had deposited the can in the collection area, he turned to his little assistant and said, "Thank you, Amanda, and have fun today."

A moment later Stuart Williams skidded to a stop within inches of Elliot. Stuart and Danny were classmates. They were also friends—some of the time. This, Elliot decided, could be one of those times. Or it could be just a visit from Stuart to boast about what appeared to be a big, shiny new bike overloaded with added accessories. "Hi, Mr. Hopper," Stuart said as Elliot walked to the car.

"Hi, Stuart."

"You don't have to take out your own garbage, do you?" Stuart commented in horror. "We pay people to do that for us. Anyway, I wanted to show Danny my new bike."

"How surprising," Elliot said mockingly. "You mean to say that you have a new possession and actually want to show it off? That's unusual for you."

"Yeah," Stuart agreed, "but you can't get this kind of bike without connections. It's a lot faster than Danny's. It cost at least twice as much, so it should be faster."

"Really?" Elliot replied. "I thought I saw one like this for sale at K mart last week."

"That couldn't be," Stuart said indignantly.

"Maybe it was Target," Elliot said, shrugging. "Anyway, your good buddy Danny is inside."

Stuart went off, and Elliot climbed into the car. "Look out, Diane!" he yelled, pretending to shield his face.

Diane grinned and started the engine. She was about to pull away when she and Elliot heard the sound of a whistle. "You're being called," she remarked good-naturedly.

"Hey," Joan Bankhead called from her yard.

"You whistled," Elliot called back, smiling.

"Hi, Elliot."

"Hi to you."

"You grown-ups have a way with words," Diane whispered.
"How's your book coming?" Elliot called.
"Very slowly. Say, I see you've got a chauffeur now."
"Well, nobody wants to live forever."
Laughing, Joan said, "You're so funny."
"Not really."
"Yes, you are."
"You're a fun person."
Diane leaned on the car horn until Elliot pulled her off it. "I'm ready to barf," she said. "Your talk is grossing me out."
Turning quickly to Joan, Elliot called, "I have to go. Are we still on for the banquet Wednesday night?"
"Wouldn't miss it for the world."
"Great."
"Buckle up, lover boy," Diane said, just before she hit the gas pedal.
When they had gone a few blocks, Diane said, "Don't you still love Mom?"
"Hey," Elliot said, "your mom wouldn't want me to be in mourning for the rest of my life. She'd want me to go out."
"Are you telling me Mom would want you to be loving it up with Joan?"
"Watch your language, young lady."
Diane shook her head in disgust. "I'm seventeen now," she complained, "and you tell me that loving it up is bad language. I can't believe it."
"Well, maybe you're right, but try to understand this, Diane. Of course I'll always love your mom. It's been a couple of years now, but things seem to be getting back to normal again around the house. And in three days all my hard work is going to pay off. I also finally met someone I like, so you should be happy for me."
"Yeah," Diane mumbled, trying to lock her mind on driving.
They rode on in silence. Elliot realized his romance with Joan was a sore point for Diane, and probably for Danny too. Amanda didn't seem to notice. Finally Diane pulled to the curb opposite his office building. Elliot smiled at her appreciatively. Her driving was very

good. "Everything is going to be fine," he said lovingly. "Just three more days to go."

"Sure," Diane said, giving him a look of affection. "And, say, this isn't easy for me, but . . . oh, just forget it."

"Happy birthday, kiddo," Elliot said, following the words with a kiss.

Diane quickly glanced around. She didn't want anyone to see her dad kissing her. She was too old for that. "Elliot . . ." she said with exaggerated indignation.

"Sorry, I forgot," he replied mockingly, then took her hand and shook it. "Warmest personal regards."

Before Diane could toss off a response, he winked and jumped out of the car. Anxious to show the car to Jonelle and some other friends at school, Diane immediately pulled away. Elliot watched her go off as he started across the street. His mind was on Diane and a dozen other things, but it should have been on crossing safely. Had it been, he would have seen the car that had shot past a stoplight and was racing toward him.

CHAPTER 5

As soon as Diane pulled away, she switched on the radio. The music that reached her ears almost gagged her. She quickly punched the other selector switches, and the sounds seemed to go from bad to disgusting. "There must be something wrong with his hearing," she mumbled to herself.

At that moment, almost the same words were being said by the driver of the car that had almost hit Elliot. Swerving to avoid an accident, the driver had blasted his horn as he sped by, but Elliot had continued across the street, unaware of how close he had brushed with disaster.

Safely on the sidewalk in front of his building, Elliot's mind fixed on work. He had forgotten about an important meeting he had downtown later in the morning. Now he wished he hadn't given away the car, because he would have to catch a cab downtown. Elliot walked through the lobby and entered the old elevator. It was empty, and as he pressed twelve, the elevator's frayed old cables creaked.

The creaking sound meant danger, but Elliot was oblivious to it. The elevator stopped at the third floor and about a dozen men got on one by one. The men were the senior directors of Elliot's company. They were also fat, and as each one stepped on, the frayed cables seemed to groan and pop from the weight. "Hello there, Hopper," one man said to Elliot. "Going to your office?"

"Well, good morning, Mr. Seymour," Elliot said, obviously elated to be greeted by the man. "Yes, I am."

"Punch eleven for us, will you?" Mr. Seymour said. "And by the way, how are you coming on our deal?"

"We should be closing it right on schedule—tomorrow."

"Gentlemen," Mr. Seymour called out, "I trust you all know Elliot Hopper. He was the first to envision the merger, and he's been handling the negotiations."

Several men smiled at Elliot, and one slapped his arm. Then the elevator started, straining from old age and the weight of its occupants. "When we meet on Thursday," Mr. Seymour continued, "Hopper will become the youngest man to sit on the Board of Directors of either of our two firms."

Elliot didn't want to appear too excited, but he was thrilled by Mr. Seymour's announcement. It was just what he wanted to hear. His long hours and hard work were going to be rewarded. "Thanks," he mumbled to one man who had congratulated him.

"That is," Mr. Seymour added, "if he doesn't mess up between now and then."

Elliot realized Seymour was joking, but he wasn't amused. He smiled politely, and Seymour's army of stooges laughed heartily. Warmed by their response, Seymour said, "Of course, if we find out that you've been having a secret romance with Mr. Nero's wife, forget about being on the board."

The stooges laughed again, just as the elevator stopped at their floor. Seymour stepped off and held the door. As the others stepped off, Elliot said, "I don't have any worries. Have you seen Mr. Nero's wife?"

To give them a better picture, Elliot oinked. Then he laughed. No one else laughed. They were busy sneaking a look at the old man who had gotten off the next elevator. As soon as Elliot saw him, he felt sick. "Mr. Nero," he said with a gasp.

Turning up his hearing aid, the old man said, "What was that?"

"I said that I haven't seen your wife lately," Elliot replied enthusiastically.

"Yes," the old man said. "I was throwing up for days, but I'm better now."

"That's good," Elliot said quickly as the doors closed.

Elliot breathed a sigh of relief. "You were very lucky just now, Elliot," he said. "Very lucky."

Elliot didn't know how lucky he was. Because of his little pep talk to himself, he didn't hear the elevator cables snapping. He stepped off the elevator with no thought of its immediate breakneck descent toward the basement. "Nero and Collins, Imports and Exports," he said, enthusiastically reading the sign on his office door. "Allow me to introduce Mr. Elliot Hopper, your new director."

Elliot bowed jokingly before pushing open the office door. At that moment the sound of the elevator crashing shook the building, but Elliot's good luck was holding. He didn't hear a thing. Inside, he saw Carol Lane, his secretary. She was at her desk, working on a cup of coffee and a doughnut. "Good morning, Elliot," she said.

"What's going on in there?"

Months earlier Elliot had been promised that his small, dark office would be renovated. "They've finally gotten around to working on your office," Carol said. "They've just put in new windows, and everything else will be ready by the end of the day. I guess all the other offices must have been finished."

"Thanks for your vote of confidence."

"What?"

"Nothing," Elliot replied. "Let's get started. Brief me on the schedule."

He turned abruptly and headed into his office. Carol leapt up and followed after him as she leafed through her notebook. "You've got negotiations from one to four," she reported, "and a five o'clock meeting with the board."

Elliot's office was in the process of becoming a large sunlit one, but for the moment he didn't have time to notice. "Can we move the negotiations up to eleven and work through lunch?" he asked. "I'm hoping to be able to finish up everything today."

"No problem," Carol said, using what Elliot had decided was her favorite expression.

With that out of the way, Elliot glanced around. "What an office this is going to be," he said, backing up to get a better idea of its spaciousness.

Carol didn't respond. She was busy with her notebook. Besides, she had just told Elliot that his new windows were in place. She didn't know the window—the wall of glass he thought he was backing toward—was missing. And she certainly didn't know Elliot's next step would give him a free-fall to the sidewalk twelve stories below. "I love this office," Elliot exclaimed.

"There's one other thing," Carol said, prompting Elliot to stop. "You have a meeting at ten with Mr. Collins at the bank downtown."

"Oh, yeah," Elliot said as he turned to look out the missing window. "Do you want me to tell you something that is very important?"

Looking his way and not noticing the missing window, Carol said, "What is it?"

Elliot cleared his throat. Neither of them was aware of the missing window. They also weren't aware of the workers backing a huge pane of glass toward Elliot—a pane big enough to send him on his way out of the opening. "The great views, the bigger office, and the promotion are not what this is all about," he announced. "After all my years of sacrifice and putting my family on hold, my family's future will finally be secure."

With that he stepped toward Carol. The move saved him from the huge pane of glass, but he and Carol hadn't even noticed it. "You'd better not get run over by a bus before Thursday," she said jokingly.

Elliot enjoyed her joke. It was the best one he had heard all day. Nothing like that would happen to him. "Right," he said, and laughed. "And hey, you'd better call and get word to Collins that I'll be a little late. Diane has the car. I have to find a cab."

"Well, don't get run over by a cab," Carol called after him.

Elliot laughed all through his ride down on the only elevator still working. Sometimes Carol was pretty funny. He was still laughing when he reached street level. Then he became serious and raced outside. Seconds later he spotted a cab dropping off a passenger, and quickly stepped over to it. He didn't notice the elevator repairmen rushing by. He also missed the message from the man leaving the cab, who whispered, "Don't ride with him."

CHAPTER 6

"Take me to First Interstate Bank on Olive," Elliot told the cabbie.

As the driver pulled away from the curb, Elliot smiled. He had been fortunate to get a cab right away, and even luckier to get one with a driver who didn't ask for directions. Elliot wanted to think about the meeting with Collins.

A minute later Elliot glanced at the cab's speedometer. "Going kind of fast, aren't we?" he remarked.

Twisting around, the driver gave Elliot a vacant stare. For the first time Elliot noticed the man's face. He needed a shave and his eyes were bloodshot. The cigarette dangling from his lips didn't help his appearance.

Elliot began to wonder if the man staring at him understood English. His vehicle was going as fast as ever. Finally Elliot pointed at the windshield and said, "I think you might want to look at the road."

"Drop dead," the cabbie replied, proving he understood some English.

"Thanks," Elliot said. "Later."

The driver turned toward the front of his cab. Elliot relaxed slightly and looked at the man's photo license, posted on the dashboard. His name was Curtis Burch, and even though his photo was ugly and disgusting, it was accurate.

"Do you worship Satan?" the cabbie asked.

The question puzzled Elliot. For one thing, it was hard to believe it had come from the driver's mouth. For another thing, it was even harder to believe the man was asking Elliot this.

"Do I what?" Elliot said incredulously.

"Do you accept the Lord Satan as the Supreme Being? Do you accept Evil as your Salvation?"

Elliot gulped, realizing he was riding with a lunatic, and the lunatic was driving. "I've always meant to get with this Satan stuff," Elliot said softly, "but I've been so busy. You know how things like that are."

At that moment the driver didn't seem aware of Elliot or his words. His bloodshot eyes were fixed on the road ahead, and he was passing red lights faster than Elliot could count them. Finally he turned toward Elliot and smiled, showing his yellow, stained teeth. "I like you," he said. "Now, do you worship Satan?"

Elliot considered leaping from the car. No, he decided, it was going too fast. Bribery seemed like a better idea. He pulled out his wallet and said, "How much do you want to stop this thing?"

The lunatic didn't respond. He seemed to be in a trance. Oh, no, Elliot thought, he's becoming an idiot. "I'll give you twenty dollars to stop," Elliot called. "In fact, you can make that forty dollars."

The lunatic responded by stepping down on the gas pedal. "Are you a moron?" Elliot mumbled. "No, no, I take that back. Let's see, I have seventy-six dollars. You can have it all, if you please stop the cab."

The wild-eyed lunatic acted as if he hadn't heard the offer, and Elliot felt frightened. "I'll throw in the wallet," he said. "It's from Gucci. I'm sure it'll impress all your buddies in Satan's Village."

The lunatic grabbed the wallet and immediately stomped on the gas pedal.

"You stop this vehicle right now!" Elliot roared.

"Do you worship Satan?"

"Worship him?" Elliot replied, deciding to try another approach. "I *am* Satan! And *I command you* to stop!"

The news obviously distressed the madman driving, and he twisted around for another look at Elliot before he let out a terror-filled scream. Matching the scream, Elliot pointed at the bridge railing toward which the cab was racing.

The cabdriver hit the brake, but he'd acted too late. A second later they slammed into the railing. The impact dumped Elliot onto the floor, and as soon as the sounds of glass breaking and steel crunching ended, he realized he had come through the crash unmarked. He climbed up and looked into the front seat. The driver groaned but seemed all right. "Nice going, dimwit," Elliot remarked sarcastically. "You could have killed us."

The driver groaned again, and Elliot decided he had had enough of the driver and the ride. "See you around," he announced, opening his door and stepping out.

Elliot shrieked in horror and reached for something to stop his fall. The cab was dangling precariously over the edge of the bridge, and Elliot was headed for a plunge in the river far below. He managed to grab the door handle and lock his grip on it.

Taking pains to move carefully, Elliot slowly inched his way back into the cab and slumped into the backseat. "Why do things like this have to happen to me?" he asked no one in particular as he shifted his position.

The car leaned with his movement, and the driver screamed. Elliot immediately shifted back to his previous spot, and the cab moved with him. "Okay," he told the driver, "now try to be calm."

"Yes, Evil Master."

Elliot couldn't believe his ears. The man was definitely a moron. There was no sense in trying to pretend he was only a lunatic. Elliot cautiously eyed the driver, who eyed Elliot's wallet on the front passenger seat. "Master," he said, reaching across the seat, "your wallet."

"No! Don't move!"

"It's a Gucci," the driver said, continuing to lean across the seat.

"No," Elliot cried, "it's a fake—an imitation. It was made in Hackensack."

Oh, no, Elliot thought as the cab slid sideways slightly before slanting toward the river. A moment later it slammed into the water and disappeared below the surface.

Elliot wasn't sure, but he guessed he had passed out when the cab hit the water. He didn't remember waking, and he certainly couldn't remember getting out and swimming to dry ground. He had done it, though, and he had climbed all the way back to the scene of the crash. He felt exhausted.

Struggling to catch his breath, Elliot spotted a cop standing by the broken railing. "Officer," he called, "it was terrible. The car is underwater."

The cop didn't respond. His face appeared to be twisted in pain. "It was bad," Elliot said, "but there's another guy down there—the driver. He must have drowned. He worshiped the devil."

This time the cop twisted toward Elliot and threw up. Elliot jumped back—too late. "What's the matter with you?" he said. "You're not supposed to fall apart when things like this happen. I'm reporting you, pal, for puking on an accident victim."

The cop gagged again and lurched toward Elliot. "That's it for you, buddy," Elliot announced angrily as he jumped back into the roadway.

A split second later he sensed something behind him and whirled around. The bus plowed into him almost as soon as he caught a glimpse of it.

The event was a momentary nightmare for Elliot, until he realized that half of his body seemed to be inside the bus. He was in the aisle, looking at the passengers, but they had no idea he was moving past them. The next thing he knew, he was standing in the middle of the road—alone. The bus had gone through him.

Watching the bus roll away, Elliot didn't want to consider the thought creeping into his head. Finally he realized he couldn't forget about what had just happened. "Oh, no!" he screamed as the thought turned into reality. "Oh, no!"

CHAPTER 7

While Elliot struggled to face his new situation, Diane struggled to face the front right fender on her birthday present. "Jonelle," she whispered to her friend, "tell me it's not dented."

"Well," Jonelle said soothingly, "it's not dented real bad."

"Great!" Diane roared, kicking at the stanchion she had accidentally hit. "Can you tell me how a flimsy steel pole like this one could dent the fender of a car?"

"I don't know." Jonelle shrugged. "But I heard that cars like yours weren't too hot in accidents."

" 'Not too hot' is an understatement. I barely bumped that pole. You know that."

"I certainly do, and I'm willing to tell your father."

"Elliot! If he even sees the dent, my days of driving are over. I have to get it fixed—right now. Is that possible?"

"No."

"Why not?"

"Well, for one thing, I don't think people in body shops are just sitting around with nothing to do. For another thing, you probably don't have the money to pay for the repairs, even if we were able to find someone who would fix it. And don't even bother to ask what you're thinking about asking. I'm broke."

"I was going to ask if you knew anybody with money," Diane said. "You're always broke."

Jonelle laughed. "Sorry for laughing," she said, "but you know me as well as I know you. We're just like sisters."

"Yeah, so you can go home and tell Dad the bad news."

"Let's not give up yet," Jonelle remarked cheerfully.

For a while the two of them leaned against the car and pondered possible solutions. "What about the shop at school?" Diane finally asked.

"The waiting list is three months long. I know for sure because Ralph Curcio told me last week."

"Ralph Curcio!" Diane said, and her eyes brightened. "He might be interested in helping me."

"Outrageous," Jonelle replied, and they both laughed.

Ralph wasn't the grossest guy in Union Hill High, but he was right up there with the top-ten weirdos. Spitting at other students in the cafeteria was his idea of fun. Still, there were some good things to be said about Ralph. For one, he liked Diane. For another, he was supposed to be great at car repairs.

"I'm going to invite him to sit with us during lunch," Diane said. "He might be able to tell us what to do."

"He might be able to tell *you* what to do. My car isn't dented. I just hope you don't have to go out with him for his help."

"Are you kidding? That would be worse than telling Elliot. Say, we'd better get moving before our independent-study time is gone."

Once they were seated in the library, Diane found she couldn't study. The dented fender occupied her thoughts. Her father certainly wouldn't like it, but would he notice it? He was so occupied with his work that he didn't seem to notice many things lately. And even though she wanted to kid herself and show off her birthday present, she knew he had forgotten all about her birthday. Still, she loved him, and he loved her. He was under a lot of pressure at work. It showed, and Diane didn't want to add to it by making him think his daughter couldn't drive safely. She would get the car fixed, if she could.

"No way," Ralph Curcio said as soon as he looked at the fender.

"You did some job on it. Your old man will probably ground you for life."

"Thanks, Ralph," Jonelle said sarcastically. "My friend needed some inspirational words from you. A belated birthday wish but very nice of you."

"What is she talking about?" Ralph asked.

"Nothing, it's just that you were the only hope I had."

"Well, I can make it look a lot better than it does now, but it's not going to look perfect."

"How bad will it look, Ralph?" Jonelle said, weakly imitating Johnny Carson.

"It'll look repaired." Ralph shrugged. "I wouldn't want anyone to know I did it because I like to keep my reputation."

"I won't tell anybody," Diane promised, "and neither will Jonelle."

"That's right, Ralph. Our lips are sealed."

For a moment Ralph stared distrustfully at Jonelle. Then he said, "I'll fix the fender for you after school, Diane. Drive over to my house. I have tools in the garage. Come alone. My mom doesn't like girls hanging around me."

"Does that happen a lot?" Jonelle said, wide-eyed.

"I'll be there alone, Ralph," Diane quickly replied.

"See you then," Ralph said and started to walk away.

"How much is it going to cost?" Diane called after him.

"I'm doing it as your birthday present," Ralph called back.

As soon as he was out of earshot, Diane whirled toward Jonelle and said, "'Does that happen a lot?' I couldn't believe you said that."

"I couldn't contain myself. 'Mom doesn't like girls hanging around me.' Ralph does have his problems."

Diane laughed. "Yeah," she agreed, "but he's sort of sweet. He's giving me a terrific birthday present."

"You didn't see it yet," Jonelle said cynically before adding, "But I think the fender will probably look great. Guys around school say that Ralph is number one at working on cars."

Later that day Diane became convinced about Ralph's ability with cars. Using some tools she had never seen before, Ralph managed to reshape the fender into nearly new condition. "These paint chips," he said, pointing, "are something you'll have to live with. I don't trust touch-up paint. It doesn't always match."

"You did a wonderful job," Diane said, hugging him enthusiastically.

They were in Ralph's driveway, and he pushed Diane away as fast as he could. His embarrassed look made Diane feel sorry about her spontaneous gesture. "I guess I got a little carried away," she said apologetically, "but I do appreciate what you've done."

"Okay," Ralph replied, "but don't tell anybody. You promised."

"I won't. You have my word."

With that Diane quickly climbed into the car and took off. She was supposed to meet her father outside his office and take him home. Judging by the time, she decided she would be late if traffic was heavy, but her dad was rarely on time, either.

As she rode, she thought about the help Ralph had given her. He was a lot nicer than she and Jonelle had thought. In fact, he was shy. Maybe, Diane thought, he spit at people because he was shy. Then she laughed at the idea. He wasn't weird. She was. She laughed again, but one thought about the day's events stuck in her mind: It was amazing how much you could learn about a person—by accident.

CHAPTER 8

Unlike Diane, Elliot Hopper wasn't happy with what he had learned by accident. Since the bus had plowed through him, he had been wandering around town trying to coax himself into facing the matter head-on. With the afternoon coming to an end, Elliot realized he had no choice. Get on with it, he told himself as he stepped over to the mirrored wall of a downtown building.

As people passed the wall they checked out their reflections. Some looked to see how they had come through a busy workday, while others looked to see how beautiful or handsome they appeared. When Elliot looked, he just hoped he appeared—in any condition. Unfortunately he made no reflection.

"Okay," he said, "I know I have to come right out and admit that I'm dead. Well, I just sort of said it. Okay, I am dead."

Elliot was calm for a moment, letting the idea sink in. Then he screamed. "I hate the idea! I don't see how I'm going to get used to it!"

Elliot stopped. No one was listening. People were just passing him by, not paying a bit of attention. He trotted over to a group of businessmen and made faces at them. He even ridiculed the way one guy was walking, but no matter how hard he tried, he couldn't get a response from anyone. That just didn't seem right.

"I don't understand why they don't give you a warning," Elliot said sadly. "They don't come and whisper, 'Skip the oat bran; it can't help you.' No, that would be the nice way to do it. I could have enjoyed a few good breakfasts. I could have finished cleaning up the garage. I was going to order those tapes and learn Japanese in the car, but I thought I had more time. So I didn't learn Japanese. I could be dead without it. I am dead! I just don't think it should have been like this. I thought people would be wearing white robes and playing harps. Instead I get a policeman in blue signaling my demise by barfing on me."

Elliot paused, recalling something he had once seen in *Reader's Digest* about self-pity being destructive. "Wait a minute!" he told himself. "You're looking at this death stuff all the wrong way. You need to examine the good side of it. You're invisible. Your son Danny would love to be invisible. Danny! Oh, no, I forgot all about the kids!"

Elliot immediately decided to go home. He knew it was a long walk, but he wasn't going to let that stop him. After all, the walk wouldn't kill him.

After a few blocks Elliot stopped. "What am I doing?" he asked. "Oscar Malin, that boring jerk who lives up the street from us, works around here. He should be getting off in a while. I'll ride with him."

It didn't take Elliot long to find Malin's car, step through the passenger door, and sit down. As he waited, he chuckled to himself. Malin was in for the ride of his dull life.

When Oscar Malin got into his car fifteen minutes later, he had every reason to believe he was alone. After starting the car he flipped on his cassette player. He was anxious to hear more of the taped book he had started listening to that morning—*Laying Your Retirement Nest Egg*.

Elliot needed two minutes of listening. After that he reached over and ejected the cassette. "My retirement eggs have been cooked," he remarked.

Elliot's move startled Malin, but he'd had trouble with the player before, so he immediately pressed the tape back into operation. A second later it jumped out of the player and sailed into the backseat.

"That did it!" he said. "That lousy dealer is going to replace the player. I'm not listening to any more of his garbage about it needing an adjustment."

Malin tuned the radio to a talk show. The subject under discussion was "rude cabdrivers." Elliot reached and switched to a music station. Malin shook his head in disgust and dialed the talk show again. Elliot leaned over and pressed on the horn. Malin slapped the steering wheel, and Elliot responded by stopping with the horn and turning off the radio. "He's going to replace the car," Malin grumbled.

They rode on, and Elliot directed his thoughts to the kids. His death was going to come as a big shock to them. He understood. He wasn't over it himself—yet. The blast of a police siren interrupted his thoughts. He turned and saw the cruiser with its blinking red light. The driver wanted Malin to pull over.

"What is it?" Malin asked as soon as the police officer stepped up to his door and glared at him.

"You were blowing your horn back there. Don't tell me you don't know anything about our anti-noise ordinance."

"I know about it," Malin replied. "I'm all for it, but I can't do much about a horn that goes off by itself."

"Oh," the police officer said, looking at Malin like he was a mental case, "it went off by itself. How interesting. Was it upset by the traffic?"

"Now see here, Officer, I am not crazy. I was driving along and the horn sounded. Maybe there's a short in the system. I don't know, but I'll take the car in tomorrow and find out. Believe me, I'm sorry about the noise."

"All right," the officer replied, "and I'm sorry for not believing you at first. It's been a long day. Anyway, good evening."

As the officer walked off, Elliot reached for the horn. Then he stopped. He wanted to get home. It would be fun to see Malin handcuffed and hauled off, but it wouldn't help Elliot. He reached over and turned on the radio. The news was on, telling about an accident by the bridge. Malin switched to another station. "Hey," Elliot cried out, "I was listening to that!"

Malin didn't hear a word Elliot said, and he didn't seem to care about the radio changing stations for no reason. He just kept switching back to the station he wanted. Finally Elliot gave up, deciding Malin was simpleminded as well as boring.

For the rest of the ride Elliot focused on giving Malin a safe and sane send-off, finally opting to settle for a safe one. As the car was about to pass his house Elliot turned off the engine. Malin braked to a stop, and Elliot threw the shift lever into park and removed the keys from the ignition. "What the devil is happening?" Malin called, boiling with frustration.

Elliot stepped through the car door, allowing Malin to see his keys seemingly sail through the window. Malin immediately slid across the front seat and got out on the passenger side in pursuit of his keys.

By then Elliot was stepping through the car, holding the keys down low so that they appeared to be running on the ground under the car. From a kneeling position Malin saw the keys. He watched as they slid inside the muffler clamp and seemed to lock there. "Don't get dirty," Elliot said, "and don't touch the muffler. It's hot."

While Malin wondered if there was something a lot more wrong with his car then he had imagined, Elliot headed for his house. When he got to the front door, he reached for the knob, but his forward motion sent him right through the door. He paused and listened. "Hey, Amanda," Danny said, his voice carrying from the den, "take a look at this. Mr. Malin is crawling under his car, and he's wearing a suit. He must be out of his mind. Dad always says he's out of his mind."

"Dad always *said,*" Elliot corrected, puzzling how he could break the news to Amanda and Danny.

CHAPTER 9

"Forget about Mr. Malin," Amanda told her brother. "This is exciting."

Elliot tiptoed to the den. As he got closer he could hear the TV playing. He quietly stepped into the room, which was dark except for the flickering television screen. Amanda and Danny were on the floor in front of it, watching intently. "What's going to happen to them?" Elliot asked himself. "Who is going to take care of them?"

Turning from the TV, Danny said, "Hi, Dad."

"Hi, Dan . . ." Elliot began.

"Hi, Daddy," Amanda added, smiling up at him.

"You're home early for a change," Danny remarked. "That's nice."

Elliot's jaw dropped. What had happened to them? They seemed all right, yet they could see him. "You can see me?" he asked tentatively.

"What was that, Dad?" Danny said, staring at him.

"You can see me?" Elliot repeated. "This is fantastic! I'm on my way back. Maybe I'm not even officially dead."

"Dad," Danny said, "what are you talking about?"

"I'm asking you if you can really, honestly see me?"

Danny frowned. "Not funny," he said. "Moving your mouth and

not saying anything isn't much of a joke. Besides, I know there's nothing wrong with my hearing, because we've been listening to the TV for over an hour."

"Not funny," Amanda agreed.

"You really can't hear me?" Elliot said, wondering if he had lost his mind when his body came back.

"What's wrong with Daddy?" Amanda asked.

"That's what I'd like to know," Diane called into the den. "I was supposed to pick him up after work but he didn't show. His secretary told me she hadn't seen him since this morning."

By the time Diane mentioned Elliot's secretary she had reached the den. "Where were you?" she asked her father as she hit the light switch.

Diane and the others jumped in fright. Elliot was gone. "Now where did he go?" Diane asked.

"Daddy?" Amanda cried out.

"What are you two talking about?" Elliot said. "I'm right here."

"That's amazing," Diane remarked. "He just vanished."

"Dad," Danny called, "that's a fabulous trick. Where are you?"

"I'm right here!" Elliot replied in a tone that reflected his frustration.

"I got it!" Danny said enthusiastically. "Diane, turn off the light."

Diane hit the switch, and like clockwork Elliot appeared.

"Excellent trick!" Danny said, adding a vocal imitation of a cheer from a crowded grandstand.

Danny's interest in magic kept him from sitting still. He rushed over to the light switch and flicked it on and off. Elliot disappeared and reappeared as fast as Danny could flip the switch.

"I don't like it," Amanda protested.

"It's obviously based on some sort of optical illusion," Danny speculated, continuing to flip the switch.

"I hate the whole thing," Diane told Danny, "so would you please stop with the lights?"

Danny stopped with the switch in the off position, and the look on Elliot's face indicated he had thought of something. Diane got the idea as soon as he pointed to himself. "I," she called out, getting the first word in the game of Charades Elliot seemed intent on playing.

Elliot smiled and nodded his agreement. Next he signaled for a small word.

"Have a very small," Diane called.

Elliot immediately repeated his signal.

"I *am*," Danny concluded.

After nodding in approval, Elliot went into what he thought was a clear, simple imitation of a ghost raising his arms and pretending to float.

"A fish!" Amanda called.

"A modern dancer!" Diane added.

Elliot shook his head and tried the imitation again, adding more emphasis to his floating.

"A big sissy!" Amanda called.

Not wanting to be outdone, Danny called, "You're an owl! You're a bat! You're a river rat!"

Elliot gestured excitedly for them to stop. He was dead and his kid was driving him crazy. The whole thing seemed to be getting out of hand. After rejecting the idea of turning on the light, Elliot pulled off his jacket and draped it over his head.

"You're a transvestite!" Danny called, and Diane threw a pillow at her brother.

"Isn't a vest some kind of clothing?" Amanda asked.

Elliot tossed the jacket aside and tugged at his earlobe. His kids recognized the signal immediately. In response he pretended to be raising a wineglass.

"Sounds like a glass," Amanda suggested.

"A drink," Diane said.

Elliot shook his head and pretended to be toasting someone with his glass.

"Sounds like *toast,*" Diane guessed.

Elliot's enthusiasm excited Diane and the others. They were getting close. The game was getting interesting.

"You want to boast," Danny called.

"No," Amanda said as her daddy shook his head, "you're a ghost!"

Elliot jumped with joy, but Diane and Danny seemed puzzled.

"You're a ghost?" Diane mumbled.

"He's a ghost!" Danny said, expecting to learn how to pull off the same trick for his friends.

Elliot went on, holding his hands as if they were on a steering wheel.

"You were driving a car," Diane said first.

Nodding appreciatively, Elliot bounced his head up and down rapidly.

"And you went over something!" Diane excitedly added.

The game tension heightened. Diane and the others sensed they were close to a solution. They could almost smell victory as Elliot held his nose and puffed up his cheeks.

"Something stinks!" Amanda guessed.

"No," Danny said, "you went into the water."

"Yes," Diane agreed. "You had an accident and went into the water."

Elliot felt thrilled. They were moving toward victory like a precision machine. He and his kids were a team—moving like champions. Folding his arms over his chest, he closed his eyes and tried to appear as stiff as a dead body.

"You drowned!" Danny said eagerly. "That's it! You're a ghost! You're dead!"

For a moment Elliot jumped with joy, and the kids shared his enthusiasm. Then the details of their discovery seemed to hit home. Their smiles disappeared.

Elliot halfheartedly tried to soften the shock with one more attempt at his ghost imitation. It fell flat. The game was definitely over. He carefully eyed Amanda. She seemed to be puzzling over the abrupt change in her sister and brother. All of a sudden she shuddered with fright and ran to Elliot, raising her arms for him to reach out and pull her to him with a big hug.

Amanda's attempt at jumping into her daddy's arms was a heartbreaking event. Like a loving daddy, Elliot reached for her just before she passed right through him and fell to the floor. Sadly he looked down at his little girl on the floor crying. "Oh, Amanda," he said, though no one could hear.

Danny and Diane rushed across the room and picked up their weeping sister. "Is Daddy going away, like Mommy?" she asked.

Diane flashed a don't-answer look at Danny. She didn't think either of them really knew the answer, but she didn't want her brother to make some flip remark that might upset Amanda even more. Danny's eyes immediately told her he agreed, and they both turned toward their dad.

Elliot was shaking his head with determination. He wasn't going away. He wanted to make that clear. He wanted to make a lot of things clear. He could feel his rage building.

"Dad," Danny said, "try telepathy. I read somewhere that ghosts communicate with telepathy. You can do it! Just concentrate!"

"We're with you!" Diane added, immediately concentrating.

Danny and Amanda joined their sister, thinking hard about making the communication work.

Seeing this show of support, Elliot decided to try. He closed his eyes, and within a few seconds his face twisted into an expression of deep concentration.

CHAPTER 10

Minutes later Elliot groaned. Diane, Danny, and Amanda opened their eyes. "Okay," Elliot's voice said, "now we're testing—one, two, three."

"I hear it," Diane reported.

"Me too," Danny added, wondering if being a ghost had something to do with ventriloquism.

"That's just great," Elliot's voice said, and again his lips did not move, though this time his facial expressions and hand movements seemed to go with the words. "Now I know this is confusing, but be patient."

"Dad," Diane said, "this is so weird. Could you move your lips, or is there something wrong with them?"

"Concentrate," Danny suggested.

Clearing his throat as he attempted to follow Danny's suggestion, Elliot said haltingly, "I am moving my lips as I speak. How do I look and sound?"

Diane and Danny exchanged worried glances. He sounded like a robot—a malfunctioning one at that. "Good," Diane said, forcing a smile.

Joining her, Danny said, "Yeah, Dad, you're doing great."

"That bad, huh?" Elliot said without moving his lips. "Well, listen to this: I am really getting the hang of it now."

"That's a little better," Diane said weakly.

Elliot tried again and again. Finally he decided to explain his repeated efforts. "Look," he said, "I know this is a little peculiar, but between now and Thursday we have to make sure no one catches on to my being a ghost."

"What good is that going to do?" Diane asked.

"You can't get life insurance after you're dead," Elliot explained. "The same is true for a pension plan. Companies are very strict about things like that. So we just have to make it to Thursday, and then you kids will be taken care of."

"I don't believe this," Diane said matter-of-factly.

"Are you going to go away like Mommy did?" Amanda asked.

Elliot bent down toward Amanda, taking care that she wouldn't go through him. "No, sweetie," his voice said. "I'm not going anywhere. I'm staying right here."

It was almost as if Elliot had uttered some magic words—dangerous magic words. A second later his body lifted off the floor and he started floating up and out of the room. "Whoa! Stop!" he called, trying to grab for something to disrupt his movement.

Diane, Danny, and Amanda watched in shocked silence. When their dad passed through the ceiling and out of the house, they ran to the window and looked for him.

After a while it was obvious Elliot was gone. Diane wrapped her arm around Amanda and closed her eyes. Danny stared out the window. Stunned by the unexpected disappearance of his dad, he brushed off the tears forming in the corners of his eyes. Maybe, he tried to convince himself, Dad will come back.

When Diane opened her eyes, she smiled and said, "Don't look so worried, Amanda. Daddy has to get used to being a ghost. You saw how he had to concentrate to talk with us. He needs to do the same thing about flying, and he will. It may take a while, but he'll be back. Until then we have to be sure that no one finds out about—"

The phone interrupted Diane. "Is that Daddy?" Amanda asked.

"I'll get it," Danny announced.

"I don't think it could be Daddy," Diane said, secretly wishing it was Elliot.

"Hello, Danny," Joan said. "Is your dad around?"

"It's Joan," Danny whispered, holding his hand over the receiver. "Should we tell her about what's going on?"

"No!" Diane said emphatically.

"Danny, did you hear me?"

"Oh, yes, Joan," Danny replied, "I just wanted to make sure my dad hadn't sneaked in without my seeing him. Anyway, he isn't home yet—probably working late at the office as usual. Do you want me to leave a note for him to call you?"

"A note," Joan said, thinking. "No, I guess not. I'll try to catch up with him tomorrow."

"Okay," Danny said, smiling wickedly at Diane, "but if he comes flying in soon, I'll have him call you."

As soon as Danny put down the receiver Diane said, "Sometimes I think you are crazy, Daniel. How could you joke about this?"

Glancing at Amanda, Danny replied, "I thought it might be a good idea."

"He may fly in soon," Amanda said sincerely.

"Yeah," Diane agreed, winking at Danny, "but we still have to keep this matter a secret. Joan doesn't know Daddy can fly."

"Right," Amanda agreed, "so you keep quiet, Danny."

"I think I'll order some pizza for our dinner," Diane said, realizing it was getting late.

Amanda and Danny immediately voiced approval of the suggestion, and Diane called in the order. A second later the phone rang again and Diane answered.

"Hi, this is Carol Lane," Elliot's secretary said. "Is your father home? I haven't heard from him, and I really should go home."

"I should have called you," Diane replied, thinking of Elliot's repeated concerns about Thursday, "I'm terribly sorry. My dad called and said that he had stopped at a quiet place to consider everything that might happen on Thursday. He said he'd be home late."

"That's strange," Carol said, sounding puzzled.

"Well, you know how my dad is. He does a lot of strange things."

"Yes," Carol agreed, though still bewildered, "I guess so. Just tell him I'll see him tomorrow."

"I'll tell him you called, Carol."

Amanda had gone off to look at the TV, so as soon as Diane put down the receiver, Danny whispered, "What if he doesn't come back?"

"I don't want to think about that. No matter what happens, we have to hold out until Thursday. Now there's a day he's not going to miss if he can help it."

"And if he does miss it?"

"I just got through saying I don't want to think about it, Danny. On Thursday we can start worrying about it."

Danny didn't argue, and Diane changed the subject by telling him about how she had dented the car fender. Once she finished the story he immediately rushed outside to check the repair work. "It looks good to me," he reported when he returned.

The sound of the doorbell cut off Diane's reply. As she guessed, it was the pizza. "Made it to you on time," the deliveryman said with a proud, wild-eyed look on his face. "And believe me, I really had to fly to do it."

Giving him a good tip along with the payment, Diane said, "Thanks, but I'm sure you didn't fly. You don't arrive in a car when you fly."

The deliveryman took his money and departed, thinking there was no sense in getting into a discussion with the girl. He had delivered there before, and the girl's father was even weirder. They gave good tips, though.

After dinner Danny recalled the fender and said, "I don't think you even have to tell Dad about it."

"I *am* going to tell him," Diane replied. "I wouldn't want him to think I was hiding it from him."

"I guess you're right," Danny agreed. "I just wish he would get here soon."

"So do I," Diane replied, but she was beginning to wonder if she would get to tell Elliot anything—ever again.

CHAPTER 11

Not long after Elliot had appeared to fly off, he found himself floating through the ceiling of another house. He didn't know how far he had traveled, but as he dropped slowly into a room that appeared to be someone's study he glanced at the books lining the wall and guessed he was far from home.

Elliot came to rest, landing gently on a large oak desk. Stretched out there, he spotted a tall, middle-aged man busy doing some paperwork. As he looked up from his work the man smiled cordially at his confused guest and said in a distinct British accent, "Hello there, Mr. Hopper, be with you in just a moment."

Elliot didn't respond. He just watched the man, who seemed to be rushing to complete his paperwork. Finally the man looked toward Elliot and said, "Be a good fellow and get off the desk, won't you?"

As soon as Elliot was off the desk, he brushed off his clothing and looked around. The room certainly didn't match any idea he had ever had about heaven, but he was sure he could get used to it. Besides, he *had* to get used to it.

A minute or so later the British-sounding chap pulled out a folder and, after briefly studying its contents, smiled at Elliot and said, "Awfully glad to have you here, Mr. Hopper. By the way, when did you die?"

Concentrating hard, Elliot said, "This morning."

"Say, old chap, you're not at all in synchronization."

The man opened his briefcase and pulled out two electrical leads with rubber tips on the end of each lead. He held the tips out to Elliot and said, "Be a good fellow and put these on your forefingers."

Elliot wanted to laugh out loud, but he held off. Heaven definitely wasn't what he had imagined. He slipped his fingers into the tips and watched as the man seemed to be adjusting some dials on his briefcase. "Now, when did you die?" the man asked.

Again Elliot concentrated and said, "This morning."

The words sounded clearer, and the man adjusted the dials once more and said, "Cause of death?"

"I drowned in a taxicab," Elliot said perfectly.

The man removed the rubber tips on Elliot's fingers and glanced at him. Elliot couldn't hide his pleasure. He beamed at his success, until the man insulted him by laughing. "I'm really quite sorry," the man said, seriously attempting to contain his laughter. "And where did this peculiar tragedy take place?"

"U.S.A. Planet Earth. By the way, this is heaven, right?"

"Don't be silly," the man replied as he selected some medical instruments, seemingly for use on Elliot.

"Then this is hell?" Elliot said with some trepidation.

"Oh, thank you very much," the man said irately. "Do I come into your home and tell you it's reminiscent of some sort of inferno? Do I tell you it is some stinking, sweltering cesspool?"

Without waiting for an answer the man went to work on measuring Elliot's head with some calipers. "Stand very still while I do this," he warned.

Elliot stiffened at the command and said, "Where am I?"

"You're in London, old bean."

While Elliot realized the man's answer went a long way in explaining his accent, he couldn't think of another thing it explained. While he puzzled over the response the man went about his business of making measurements of Elliot and writing them down.

Finally Elliott said, "Excuse me, sir, but this has been an extraordinary day for me, so I wonder if you'll be kind enough to answer one little question — what am I doing in London?"

"Acting just like an American, I'm afraid," the man announced as he stepped away from Elliot. "Left our good manners, 'home, home on the range,' have we?"

"What am I doing here?" Elliott replied, unable to hide the rage building within him.

"Actually I summoned you here. I sensed a disturbance in the spirit ether, which is always a sure sign of intercorporeal maltransference."

"A what?"

The man picked up a device that looked like one of those treasure detectors Elliot had seen advertised in magazines and started running it over Elliot's body. "It means that they seemed to have screwed up," the man explained as he wrote down his readings from Elliot's body. "It's the afterlife equivalent to misplacing your paperwork. It's rare, but it happens. Anyway, it's what you might call a specialty of mine. I've written *the* book on it."

To support his point the man showed Elliot a book titled *On Intercorporeal Maltransference.* Elliot took note of the author's name—Sir Edith Moser. "Very interesting," Elliot remarked.

"Glad you think so. Now let's get on with my research."

"No," Elliot said, "I've got to go back. You have the power to send me back, don't you?"

"Why, of course I can send you back, but why, pray tell, would I want to?"

"Listen, after Thursday I'll come back and you can research every inch of my dead body."

"Thursday? You really must excuse me if I laugh."

"What's so funny?"

"You're in a temporary state right now," the Englishman explained. "I've never known anyone to last more than three days in your condition, and most go in less."

The news caught Elliot off-guard. "What happens then?" he said hesitantly.

"The endless snooze, I'm afraid."

"That settles it," Elliot replied. "I have to make it to Thursday."

"Well, your readings are strong. Have you started to flicker yet?"

"Not that I know of."

"You might make it to Wednesday, even that night, but not to Thursday. That's quite impossible."

Elliot stopped. The man had sort of pronounced his death sentence, except for one thing—Elliot was already out of it. In the meantime, though, he had to do something for Diane and the others. "I must go back and try," he asserted. "It's for my kids. They are so young, and their momma died a few years ago and I'm all they've got. What do you say, Sir Edith?"

"Eh-dith," he said, correcting Elliot's pronunciation. "The first syllable has a short sound."

"I would have bet it should sound like its name," Elliot said, "but either way, it's a girl's name."

"See here, Eh-dith is *not* a girl's name. I should know."

"I'm sorry. How did you get the name?"

"I was named after my grandmama."

"Your grandmother was called Eh-dith?"

"No, her name was Ee-dith. The first syllable was an *E* and was sounded like it."

"So that proves you have a girl's name."

"I do not!" Sir Edith said. "Now please stand still so I get your measurements right."

"No," Elliot protested, moving from side to side. "You've got to send me back. I can't let my kids down again. Please."

Frowning slightly, Sir Edith said, "All right, I'll send you back, but I'm going to need you for further readings. Do we have a deal, as you Americans say?"

"Sure. Whatever you want."

"Off you go, then. Godspeed."

Then Sir Edith pushed a button on one of his many odd-looking devices, and Elliot shot toward the ceiling. "Whoa," he called, just before he passed through the ceiling, "I don't want to get killed twice."

"I'd like to kick that man in his dead backside," Sir Edith grumbled, thinking he might have committed a terrible error by allowing Elliot Hopper to return to the U.S.A.

CHAPTER 12

"*The Cosby Show* is on now," Diane told her brother and sister. "You always say you love it, so why aren't you watching instead of staring out the window?"

"I'm waiting for Daddy," Amanda explained.

"So am I," Danny confessed.

"Just waiting around this dining room isn't going to bring him back," Diane remarked.

"You were by the window when we got here," Danny said. "Besides, I really wouldn't want to watch *The Cosby Show* now, with Dad missing. He looks a lot like Bill Cosby. Did you ever notice that?"

"Elliot?" Diane said, sneering at her brother. "When Dad gets back, I'm telling him you need your eyes checked. He doesn't look one bit like Bill Cosby."

"Yes, he does," Amanda said seriously.

Diane was just about to offer Amanda some advice about her eyes when Elliot popped through the ceiling. "Hey," he called, "look who's back."

"Dad!" Danny said excitedly.

"Daddy!" Amanda added.

Darn, Diane thought, he does look a little like Bill Cosby.

As the kids watched, Elliot waved his arms, trying hard to slow his downward motion. Nearing floor level, he braced himself somewhat for a crash landing. Instead he saw his feet passing through the dining-room floor and quickly flapped his arms, hoping to keep from disappearing once again.

Somehow Elliot managed to stop himself. Half of his body had gone through the floor, and the other half, which appeared to be sticking up out of the floor, was at an angle. Still, Elliot concluded, it was better than being in the basement.

"Are you okay?" Danny asked.

"I think so," Elliot answered, "and I'll even be better once I get used to this flying stuff."

"We thought you might—" Diane started to say.

"I know," Elliot said, interrupting, "but it's okay. I'm back."

Diane and the others eyed him with concern. He was struggling to get his legs through the floor, but their concern seemed to be about having a ghost dad. "Everything is going to be fine," Elliot lied.

"Where did you go?" Danny asked.

"I was in London with a guy named Edith."

Diane and Danny exchanged looks of obvious disbelief. "Okay," Diane said, "if you don't want to tell us where you go, that's fine with us."

Amanda's judgment wasn't as harsh. She sat on the floor and looked at the part of her daddy sticking out of the floor. "Can I take you to show-and-tell?" she asked.

"No, Amanda, you can't. I'm sorry, but that's the way it has to be. And if anyone asks, you just tell them that everything around here is perfectly normal. That goes for all of you. Okay?"

Amanda and the others nodded in agreement as the phone sounded. "I'll get it," Diane announced.

"Who could that be?" Elliot said, thinking out loud. "I guess I'm going to have to stick around here. We'll have to tell people I'm not feeling well."

"It's Mr. Collins," Diane said, "and he sounds like he's seen a ghost."

"Not funny," Elliot said as the phone she had thrust at him kept passing through his ghost hand.

"Concentrate," Danny said encouragingly.

Elliot tried, locking his mind on the phone. A few seconds later he picked it up and said, "Mr. Collins."

After explaining he was still at the office with Mr. Nero, Collins said, "Things are falling apart, Hopper. I don't know where you were all day, but there were a lot of people waiting for you, and you didn't have the good business sense to call and say you were standing them up!"

"Mr. Collins," Elliot protested weakly, "I assure you—"

Collins cut him off. "You better not blow this deal, Hopper," he said, "or perhaps you want me to recite all the mean things I will personally do to you."

"That's not necessary," Elliot said, and hung up.

"Was it bad?" Danny asked.

"Bad enough," Elliot admitted, "but it'll be a lot worse if I don't think of a way to go to work tomorrow. For now you kids can help me by going about your usual business and giving me a chance to concentrate on getting the rest of my body into this room."

An hour later Elliot called Amanda and the others into the living room. There he outlined the plan he had devised for going to work the next morning. It wasn't a spectacular plan, but as Danny remarked, "It was worth a shot."

With that out of the way, Elliot sent Amanda off to bed, after first demonstrating it was impossible for him to kiss her good night. Later, when it was time for Danny to go to bed, he held out his hand and said, "We can shake, Dad, if you concentrate."

To Elliot's surprise, concentrating on the handshake was all he needed to make it work. "Well," he jokingly told Danny, "let that be a lesson to you—handshaking is a lot easier than kissing."

When Diane was about ready to turn in, it was past eleven on the living-room clock. "Are you going to bed soon?" she asked her father.

"No, I'm beginning to think ghosts don't get tired."

"So you're going to sit up all night?"

"I guess that's my job. I'm a ghost."

"That reminds me," Diane said. "Do you really think you can go to work like this? Who are you trying to kid?"

"Hey, I'm not saying it'll be some kind of a breeze, but it can be done."

Diane watched him concentrate on a bottle sitting on the bar. "If I concentrate hard enough," he said, fixed on the bottle, "and if we all stick to the plan, we can keep people from knowing I'm a ghost."

"And if we don't?" Diane said, watching her father pour a drink for himself. "What happens to us? You don't have life insurance, and you don't own this house."

"That's all true," Elliot said sadly.

"How am I supposed to support myself and a brother and sister?"

"Diane, somehow I am going to pull this off. I give you my word—I am not going to let you kids down."

Elliot raised the glass in a toast. "When did you start drinking?" Diane asked. "I thought that stuff was for special occasions."

"Right," Elliot agreed, gesturing with the glass. "Here's to Thursday."

After bringing the glass to his lips and drinking, Elliot realized he hadn't tasted a thing. He looked down and noticed a large puddle forming on the floor.

"The drink just went right through you," Diane said sadly. "I'll see you in the morning. I need to sleep and forget what just happened."

Elliot flickered a few minutes after Diane departed. By his guess, the flickering didn't last more than a second or two, but it worried him. Had the Englishman been right? Was he going to flicker out before Thursday?

CHAPTER 13

Elliot awakened everybody early the next morning. He wanted to get an early start on their trip to the office, and he wanted the kids to have one last look at him before daylight hit and wiped him out.

At breakfast Diane reported on denting the car fender and having it repaired. Elliot tried, but he couldn't get interested in the story, though he knew he should. Finally he said, "If I get a new company car on Thursday, I'll leave it to you."

"Are you going away?" Amanda asked immediately.

"You can't leave a new company car to somebody else," Danny said firmly, before adding, "Can you?"

"Let's worry about all those things later," Elliot remarked. "For now you can worry about finishing breakfast and gathering up all of our equipment. I think I'm about to disappear."

Amanda was ready first, so Elliot decided to go to the car with her. "We'll be in the car," he called to Diane and Danny. "Now, Amanda, you take my hand, because as soon as I open the door, you won't be able to see it."

"Can I hold it?" Amanda said hesitantly, fearful that her hand would go right through his.

"Yes, I want you to hold my hand so I can practice concentrating."

As a ghost should, Elliot vanished in the daylight, but Amanda kept a tight grip on his invisible hand. She liked holding her daddy's hand.

Unfortunately Stuart Williams happened to be riding by the Hopper house at that moment, and when he glanced at it, hoping to see his friend Danny, he almost fell off his bike. Amanda seemed to be going somewhere, and she had one hand in the air. Stuart braked to a stop, wondering if Danny had switched from magic to hypnotism.

Watching carefully, Stuart saw Amanda pass an overturned bike. Then she stopped and looked at it. The bike was raised into an upright position—by itself. Or was it being moved by a ghost? Stuart rejected the thought almost as quickly as it entered his mind. He didn't believe in ghosts—especially in his own neighborhood.

"Get in," Elliot told Amanda, opening the car door for her and also getting in.

Stuart's eyes almost popped. The car door had opened and closed by itself. The bike had stood up by itself. The Hoppers were going from weird to super-weird. He fought off his instinct to call Danny, who was getting into the car with Diane. Instead he decided to watch.

"You're sitting on me," Elliot said.

Danny jumped up. "Sorry," he said. "I'll get in the back."

Once Danny was seated, Diane started the engine and took off. "I still don't think this is going to work," she announced.

Still dazed by the unexplainable things he had observed, Stuart attempted to follow the car, but in his haste he ran into a hedge. By the time he was ready to roll again, the car was gone.

Diane drove fast, but Elliot didn't complain about her speed. "Flying is really scary," he told Danny.

"I'd like to be able to do it," Danny said.

"That's just what we need," Diane said sarcastically. "Two ghosts dropping in every now and then."

After parking, they rode the elevator to Elliot's office. It was early, but Carol was there, working away. "Hi, kids," she said as Diane, Danny, Amanda, and her invisible boss went past her. "Where's your dad? Collins and the others were going crazy looking for him."

"Maybe he's dead," Diane mumbled.

"Tired!" Danny quickly added. "Dead tired."

Carol followed them into Elliot's office. "Well, what do you think of your dad's new surroundings? Pretty fancy, huh?"

The kids didn't answer. They were busy closing the drapes and turning off all the lights. "What are you doing?" Carol finally asked.

"Carol," Danny said as Elliot waved the faint outline of his hand in her face, "do you see my father anywhere?"

"No, and don't change the subject."

Danny glanced around and spotted one last light. He turned it off, and Elliot immediately came into view. "Oh, no!" Carol screamed.

"Hi," Elliot said meekly.

"You scared the lunch out of me, Elliot. Don't ever do that again."

"Sorry," Elliot replied. "I had no way of knowing you'd had lunch already."

"Where have you been? Collins is absolutely furious."

"It's a long story."

"I thought it might be."

Elliot looked around. "Okay, kids," he said, "I think this works fine. Let's lock it in."

Diane handed masking tape to Danny and Amanda. They quickly taped all the drapes shut and unscrewed all the light bulbs. In total disbelief, Carol looked from Elliot to the kids and back again.

"Okay, Carol," Elliot told her, "we have a lot to get done."

"Okay, Elliot, but first tell me what they're doing."

"I just thought it would be nicer in here without all that lousy sunshine."

"What?" Carol remarked. "I thought you loved sunshine."

"Oh, yeah. Actually, it's the view. It's not pretty, and it's very distracting."

"You told me last week you loved the view."

"It's really my eyes," Elliot said, obviously struggling. "They've suddenly become very sensitive to light."

"Well, why didn't you say so?" Carol replied. "I can buy that."

"Okay, we'll stick with that. Diane, you pick me up later. You all did good work. Excellent, as a matter of fact."

"If St. Peter calls for you," Diane joked, "we'll get the number."

"Thanks a lot," Elliot said as the three of them trooped out of the office.

Carol slid a schedule toward Elliot. "Here's what we are looking at," she said.

"Cancel the ten. Cancel the ten-thirty. Ditto the twelve, the two, the five, and both five-thirties."

"You can't cancel the five."

"What about the four?"

"You don't have a four."

"Well, move the five to four and cancel the four."

Carol wasn't sure she had heard him correctly, but she got busy writing down what she could remember. At the same time Elliot started floating out of the office.

Elliot knew the feeling. He'd had it just before his trip to England. "No!" he called out, concentrating hard on sticking around.

"Don't cancel the four?" Carol asked without looking up.

"Yes," Elliot said, "cancel the four."

"What about the six?" Carol said as Elliot struggled with the force pulling him toward the window.

"Cancel it."

The force wouldn't stop. It stretched Elliot out of shape. "Not now!" he screamed in protest.

"What do you mean?" Carol asked. "Do you want to cancel it—or not?"

Elliot managed to pull back into recognizable form just before Carol shot a look his way. "You can cancel it later at your convenience," he explained.

"Are you okay?" Carol asked, wondering why Elliot seemed to be making jerky movements with his body.

"I'm fine," Elliot replied, continuing his struggle with the force. "I don't understand why you even asked."

"Well, do you want some coffee?"

"No thanks. The stuff just seems to run right through me."

Carol couldn't take any more. Elliot was working too hard—much too hard. She put down her notebook and pulled off her glasses. "Elliot," she said, looking at him with deep concern, "forgive me, but I'm worried about you."

"You shouldn't worry. I'm all—"

"Listen," Carol interrupted as she turned her back to him. "This is hard for me to say, so just hear me out."

The force wanted Elliot, and it felt as if no amount of concentration could stop it. Elliot clenched his teeth and tried, anyway.

"When you work with someone as closely as I have with you," Carol continued, "you come to have certain feelings for that person. You . . ."

The force lifted Elliot out of the room. He didn't have time to say good-bye or even apologize for another disappearance. As he passed over Carol's head he realized she was still babbling on. *Oh, well,* he thought, *if I have to go, this is probably a good time.*

CHAPTER 14

Instead of fighting the force, Elliot relaxed and tried to enjoy the flight. He soon realized he was going too fast to enjoy anything, so he closed his eyes and thought of more things he should have done when he was alive.

Elliot's thoughts about being alive ended when the force guided him into a landing in a small, dark room. Listening to the humming sound all around him, Elliot puzzled over where he might be, but nothing came to mind. Finally he said, "Hello, is there anyone home?"

Almost like magic, a door swung open, and Sir Edith entered the small room, just about sandwiched in alongside Elliot. Before Elliot could speak, Sir Edith turned a latch on the door and a light went on inside the room, which seemed to be an airplane lavatory. "Hello, hello," Sir Edith said good-spiritedly. "How are we today?"

"*Where* are we today might be a better question," Elliot remarked irately.

"We're on British Airways somewhere over the Atlantic, I understand. I was napping before your arrival."

"You can go right back to napping after you get me out of here," Elliot said. "I have work to do."

"My dear chap, you're dead, so relax and enjoy it. No one expects you to get any work done. By the way, I can't see hide nor hair of you in this light."

"I'm right here."

Sir Edith turned and unlatched the door, triggering the mechanism that shut off the lavatory light. "Ah, that's much better," he said, facing Elliot in the darkness.

"Read my lips," Elliot said, trying to recall where he had heard that ridiculous expression. "I have to go back to my office right now. My secretary is talking to me, and she could run out of words."

Seemingly oblivious to Elliot's request, Sir Edith started measuring Elliot once again. "I don't think you appreciate how important this is," he said. "What happened with you hasn't happened in over forty years."

Elliot didn't respond. He didn't appreciate any part of what was going on. Neither did the nun who opened the lavatory door and saw two men, one appearing to be holding the other by the shoulders. "Well, excuse me," she said, quickly closing the door.

Sir Edith shrugged and continued with his work. "Your readings aren't very good," he said with concern.

"I flickered last night," Elliot confessed. "What does that mean?"

"It means you should be getting your affairs in order—quickly."

Elliot gulped. "How much time do I have?" he asked.

"A day," Sir Edith speculated, "or thirty-six hours, tops."

"That doesn't get me to Thursday."

"You might not even get to Wednesday," Sir Edith replied, "if you start playing ghost and run yourself down."

"Playing ghost? What do you mean?"

Sir Edith wiggled his fingers and fluttered his cheeks. "Oooga, oooga, booga!" he said in a ghostlike imitation. "Jumping out of walls, flying around, scaring people. Loads of fun, I admit, but very draining."

Flying around, Elliot thought, *hasn't been my idea*. "Send me back," he said. "I don't have a minute to spare, so send me back right now. You have to!"

"All right," Sir Edith said reluctantly. "I should be on the Coast by sometime tomorrow. I'll see you then, what?"

"That'll be great. Just don't whisk me away anymore! I can't take it, so use the phone. Make an appointment. Ring my bell. Stop over for a spot of tea, what?"

"You're a mite touchy, old chap, but very well. Be off now."

Sir Edith pressed the button on his case, and Elliot rocketed off. The Englishman smiled at the sight, thinking the touchy American would be back where he started before he knew it. A second later he threw open the lavatory and came face-to-face with the nun, who was cautiously awaiting her turn.

Instead of rushing into the lavatory, she waited for the other man she had seen step out. He didn't, and she could see that the room was empty. "Careful with that flush mechanism," Sir Edith warned. "It's extremely powerful."

Sir Edith promptly headed down the aisle, and by the time he reached his seat, Elliot was tumbling through the window of his office and landing on the floor. To his amazement—and delight—Carol was still looking away and talking. He struggled to get to his feet.

"These passions burn deep with us," Carol said, "but we must never even speak their name. Never! Do you understand what I'm telling you?"

With that question Carol whirled toward Elliot. "Yes," he agreed, though totally bewildered by her speech, "that's terrific! I'm with you all the way on this one! It's fantastic! Or as Danny would say—outstanding!"

Carol choked with emotion. She immediately bit her lip and rushed from the office, fighting back tears of joy. Still bewildered, Elliot promptly hit the intercom and said, "Let's get started setting up some conference calls."

"Oh," Carol's voice said, "I forgot to tell you that you have to take your life-insurance physical this afternoon."

The idea shocked Elliot and undoubtedly would have sent a chill up his spine if he still had one. "What?" he screamed at the intercom. "Can't they just give me the insurance without the physical?"

"No, and they said it's this afternoon or never. I have the forms right here."

Elliot didn't want to believe her response. He paced back and forth, formulating a plan. However, Carol wasn't waiting. She gathered up the forms, picked up her coffee, and went back to see Elliot.

"You've got to get them to waive the exam," Elliot was saying to the intercom. "Call them right now and think of something. Also make sure the paperwork for my pension plan is pushed through, will you?"

Carol gasped. Elliot was in the middle of the desk. His legs were gone, and his upper body seemed to be resting on the center of his desk. Her jaw dropped open, and she steadied her grip on the coffee cup.

"And one more thing," Elliot said, just as he realized Carol's gasp hadn't come over the intercom.

Turning and seeing the look on her face, he promptly realized where he was standing and simultaneously rejected the notion of jumping out of the desk. He didn't want to exhaust himself playing ghost. Instead he stood his ground and picked up his own coffee cup. "I think someone has been slipping some mind-bending stuff in this coffee," he remarked casually. "Have you noticed that?"

"Oh, no," Carol said, taking the suggestion faster than she could spell *relief*. "Here are the forms. I think I'm going to be sick."

Elliot reluctantly took the forms, and Carol rushed out of the office. Standing there with the paperwork in hand, he shot a glance at the wall mirror. His reflection wasn't in it, but the paperwork was. *I probably don't have a shadow, either,* he thought, and then a brilliant idea hit him.

After checking the time Elliot picked up the phone and tapped out his home number. "Diane," he said, "am I glad I caught you at home. Now go to my hall closet and get the following things and bring them to me right away. . . ." Elliot outlined his needs.

When he was finished, Diane said, "I'll be missing school."

"You'll be missing me if you don't hurry," Elliot warned, before putting down the receiver.

CHAPTER 15

Elliot's warning worried Diane. In fact, the entire matter worried her. As she gathered all the items he wanted, she wished she could tell Jonelle about Elliot, but she had promised to keep this ghost business secret. Besides, she decided, Jonelle wouldn't believe it. No one in school would believe her father was a ghost, except perhaps the school psychologist. Rumor had it that he would believe anything.

During the drive to Elliot's office, Diane decided she needed to be calm. Amanda was on the verge of becoming very upset about the situation, and Danny would also probably be quite disturbed once he got over the idea of having the best magic trick in the world for a father. So instead of worrying, Diane concentrated on the kind of excuse she was going to make for missing her calculus class.

Diane stopped in front of Elliot's office building. A second or so later, the passenger door opened and some papers floated into the car. Then the door slammed shut as several pedestrians watched in bewilderment. "Haven't they seen medical papers before?" Elliot said as he placed the papers on the seat. "Let's get out of here."

"Where to?" Diane asked as she pulled away from the curb.

After giving her the address of the medical building, Elliot fixed his attention on all the items in the backseat. "Good work," he told Diane.

"I guess it is, but what do you plan to do with those clothes? Are you planning a quick trip to Alaska?"

"I need to be seen in the daylight. The clothes I have on are ghost clothes. They became invisible when I did. Does that make sense to you?"

"Sure, but why'd you want clothes good for Chicago in January? Most people are still wearing summer clothes. Baseball season isn't even over yet."

"I need to cover every bit of me," Elliot explained as he started to dress. "A short-sleeved shirt with no arms or neck or head sticking out of it creates suspicion."

"Right, but—"

"But an eccentric man who finds this weather cold is a different story. They'll think I'm from Arizona."

Diane understood his idea. She had seen *The Return of the Invisible Man* on TV one night. "They might," Diane said, eyeing the "body" coming together in the seat alongside her, "but what are the other things for?"

Elliot quickly explained he needed them because he had to take a complete physical.

Diane laughed as she thought about how he planned to use the items. "I'm sorry," she said, continuing to laugh, "but you're becoming a crazy ghost. You really are."

"Trust me," Elliot said with assurance.

Diane parked near the entrance. Trying to keep a straight face, she watched as Elliot pulled on his galoshes and adjusted the woolen scarf covering his face. "How do I look?" he asked.

"I don't know which I like more," Diane said jokingly, "your hat or your gloves."

"Just trust me," Elliot said, opening the car door, "and be back here in two hours."

"Okay, but I'm going to miss another class."

"Can't be helped," Elliot said, slamming the door and setting out for the entrance.

For a moment Diane watched. People in summer clothes were sneaking glances at the man in the heavy overcoat. They don't think he's from Arizona, she thought, they just think he's crazy. Still, she concluded as she pulled away, crazy people needed physicals too.

The glances from people quickly became outright stares, and Elliot just as quickly decided to deal with them directly. "Brrr," he announced, rubbing his arms and glancing around, "it sure is cold here. How do you stand it?"

Caught staring, the people slunk off without a word. Elliot shrugged and stepped into the building. So far, he thought, so good.

Doctors and nurses seemed to be racing around the Oak Tree Medical Corporation. "Are you Elliot Hopper?" a female voice asked as Elliot entered the office.

Elliot saw it was a nurse directing the question to a nervous-looking middle-aged man. "No, I'm Rob Cohen," the man replied, and his eyes widened in fear as he heard the crunching of galoshes.

"Well, good that it's warmer in here. Say, I'm Elliot Hopper."

Routinely the nurse handed Elliot a clipboard with a form on it and said, "Okay, Mr. Hopper, you just take this to Room 2 and get stripped down to the waist."

Elliot took the clipboard and hurried down the hallway. As soon as he was inside Room 2 and had closed the door, he went to work, pulling off his clothing, turning down the lights, and preparing his other equipment. When he was just about ready, he heard a knock on the door. "Come on in," he called.

A doctor stepped into the room and picked up the clipboard Elliot had been given. Like the nurse at the front desk, he seemed oblivious of Elliot. After a few seconds he remarked, "Why is it so dark in here?"

"Please," Elliot begged, "I'm very shy."

The doctor shrugged and adjusted his stethoscope. Then he placed it against Elliot's chest. Smiling confidently, Elliot stood there with his hands behind his back.

In a matter of seconds the doctor's expression went from pleasure to disbelief. "Something wrong?" Elliot finally asked.

"Your heart has stopped," the doctor said incredulously.

"Must be something wrong with your stethoscope," Elliot said, starting to fumble with something behind his back.

While the doctor checked his stethoscope Elliot surreptitiously rewound the tape of a clock ticking on Danny's portable player, which he had behind his back. "Try it again," Elliot said.

This time the doctor listened for about a minute. "Must have been the stethoscope," he told Elliot. "Your heart runs just like a watch. You can go across the hall now and see Nurse Satler in X ray."

Without another word the doctor handed the clipboard to Elliot and went on his way. Elliot paused and gave a sigh of relief before pushing on to his next big hurdle—X rays.

A confident Elliot emerged from the examination room. Down the hall, a shaky Rob Cohen emerged from another examination room. Elliot waved to Cohen before he pushed open the door of the X-ray room and stepped inside.

Rob Cohen's eyes bulged, and he struggled to maintain his balance. He had just seen a clipboard cross the hall, and the clipboard had seemed to wave at him. *You're taking this physical too seriously,* he told himself, and tried to catch his breath.

To Elliot's satisfaction the room was dark. To his dissatisfaction Nurse Satler was waiting, and as soon as she took the clipboard from him, she said, "Stand behind the machine and place your chest against the plate, please."

Elliot looked for the nurse. She was behind the protective lead wall, giving all her attention to an X-ray monitor. Then Elliot looked around the room, praying it would have what he needed.

The picture on the monitor surprised Nurse Satler. "Mr. Hopper," she said angrily, "you must place your chest against the plate."

A few seconds later an X-ray image appeared on the nurse's screen. "Hands on hips," she called.

Elliot struggled with the human skeleton he had placed in front of the machine. Getting its hands on its hips wasn't easy, and the last thing Elliot wanted to do was fall apart—on camera. That would be hard to explain and would definitely raise his insurance premiums.

The image on Nurse Satler's screen puzzled her. Finally she

remarked, "Did anybody ever tell you that you've got the bone structure of a woman?"

"Just my luck," Elliot mumbled in response.

"Breathe in and hold," the nurse said, just before taking the X-ray.

"Is that it?" Elliot asked.

"That's right, Mr. Hopper. Send in the next patient and go get dressed."

Elliot smiled to himself and moved the skeleton to one side. Then he stepped to the door and opened it. "You're next, Mr. Cohen," he said.

Forgetting about the light pouring into the room, Elliot turned and pushed the skeleton into the corner it had occupied.

"Thank you," Mr. Cohen started to say, until he realized the only thing in the room was a skeleton—a moving one. He gasped for air just as Elliot realized what was wrong.

"See you later," Elliot said as he slipped past the petrified Mr. Cohen.

Elliot began dressing as soon as he was back in the room in which he had started. He couldn't wait to see Diane and tell her how he had breezed through the physical. His smart-aleck daughter had doubted him. She had almost sneered when he'd asked her to trust him. Well, she had a big surprise coming to her.

Elliot had a big surprise coming to him too. A nurse stuck her head in the door and said, "Oh, Mr. Hopper, I'm glad I caught you. There's one last thing we need from you."

She handed Elliot a capped plastic bottle. Elliot recognized it immediately. A sick expression spread across his face. "I don't know—" he started to say.

"The bathroom is down the hall," she said, interrupting, "and there's a water fountain right outside the door."

"Water," Elliot said with a gulp, "just seems to run right through me."

"Good," the nurse said, "then you won't have any trouble."

She was gone before Elliot could voice another objection. He stared at the plastic bottle. Maybe, he thought, Miss Smart-aleck was right, after all.

CHAPTER 16

Diane was leaving school when she ran into Ralph Curcio. "I guess your dad didn't notice the fender," he said.

"What makes you say that?"

"I saw you driving your car this morning, so I knew you weren't grounded."

"I'm not grounded, but I did tell him about the fender," Diane said. "He didn't think it looked bad, thanks to you. By the way, I didn't see you this morning."

"No," Ralph said, "I didn't think you did. I was in front of you over on Stockbridge Avenue. I spotted you in my mirror."

"Oh, yeah, I was taking my dad to work. I had my brother and sister with me."

"I could see them, but where was your dad?"

"Sitting next to me," Diane said, and caught herself. "I mean, he was sitting next to me after I picked him up. When you saw me, I was going to the house, where I was supposed to pick him up."

"Oh, I see what you mean," Ralph said, though he was obviously bewildered.

"Now I have to pick him up again," Diane said.

"Want me to ride along with you?"

"Are you crazy?" Diane blurted out, thinking how embarrassed she would be if he saw Elliot in his Antarctic tourist outfit.

"I'm sorry," Ralph mumbled, hurt by the sharp rejection. "I'll see you around."

"Wait a minute," Diane pleaded, moving after him. "I'd love to have you ride along with me sometime, but not when I have to pick up my father. He's a little weird lately. So I'm the one who's sorry now."

Feeling better, Ralph smiled at her and said, "That's the name of an old song Connie Francis used to sing long ago. I learned it from my mom."

"Tell me about it," Diane said, glancing at her watch. "I have a little time yet."

Meanwhile Elliot was thinking about time too. As the nurse had directed, he had walked over to the bathroom, but he was stuck there. His plastic cup was empty, and though the thought of filling it with water had entered his mind, he didn't think he could get by with water. It would be stretching his luck.

By the time Mr. Cohen walked into the bathroom with his plastic bottle, Elliot was beginning to believe he was going to fail his physical. "How are you doing?" Elliot said.

Cohen didn't reply. He seemed frightened to death by the sight of Elliot, but he was determined to complete his physical. Elliot listened with envy, half wondering if he could prevail upon the man to fill his bottle too. Then it hit Elliot—the way to pass his physical.

As soon as Cohen tightened the top on his bottle and started for the door, Elliot blocked his way. "I lose my head when I have to do things like that," Elliot said.

"Step aside, please," Cohen replied.

"Look," Elliot said, bending forward and pulling off his hat.

Cohen choked and turned pale. The man's head was gone, and it looked as if his body were gone too. "Let me out!" he screamed, dropping the plastic bottle and running around Elliot.

"Thank you very much," Elliot said, scooping up the bottle as the bathroom door slammed shut. "I just hope your kidneys are good."

Heading back to the examination room, Elliot heard a nurse say, "There goes Mr. Hopper. See, there's nothing wrong with him, Mr. Cohen. You're just a little stressed out from your physical. Now go ahead and do your tinkle and you're finished. Yes, do it again."

Elliot almost jumped into the dark room. He quickly removed his hat, coat, and gloves. Maybe, just maybe, some nurse was going to check on Mr. Cohen's claim. Elliot felt slightly sorry for the man, but nothing was going to stand in the way of his passing the physical—hopefully.

As Elliot had guessed, a nurse did appear seconds later. "Just collecting your specimen," she said, smiling broadly, "and I'm glad to see you haven't lost your head yet. Did you see Mr. Cohen in the bathroom?"

"Yes, he's a strange man," Elliot remarked.

"You're a little strange yourself," the nurse replied, looking at Elliot's clothing, "but at least you haven't gone off the deep end. Take care of yourself."

"No problem," Elliot replied.

Three minutes after the nurse departed, Elliot shot out of the room. Filled with pride at his success, he literally danced out of the medical offices into the hall. In his excitement his scarf slipped aside and his hat appeared to be floating in space. Then he turned a corner and came face-to-face with Mr. Cohen.

As soon as he saw the wide-eyed terror on Mr. Cohen's face, Elliot reached for his scarf, but it was too late. The frightened man screamed and ran off down the hall. "I'm sorry," Elliot whispered, hoping Diane would be on time.

Unfortunately Elliot was early. The physical hadn't taken as long as he had estimated, so he had fifteen minutes to waste. He amused himself by playing a little game he named It's Not Nice to Stare.

Turning on the first guy he caught staring, Elliot said, "Do I have the right time?"

Then, as the starer watched, Elliot thrust his wrist out of his jacket sleeve and revealed his watch. The starer checked the time on Elliot's watch, until he realized the watch was floating in space. Then he ran off.

The next victim was gaping at Elliot for a long time before Elliot reached down and took off his shoe, shaking an imaginary pebble from it. Realizing that Elliot didn't seem to have a foot, the gaper quickly went on his way.

Elliot was just about to throw open his overcoat for a female starer when Diane pulled to the curb. "You just saved a woman from fainting," Elliot said cheerfully as he got into the car.

"Don't even bother to explain," Diane replied. "Just tell me about your physical."

"I passed."

"How?"

While Elliot related the details of his physical, he also removed the clothes he had been wearing. In truth, he had always liked the clothes he'd died in, and having them as his ghost clothes amused him.

Diane wasn't amused with either his ghost clothes or any of the things that had happened during his physical. "Now you're invisible until dark," she complained. "That bothers me—it doesn't amuse me!"

"What are you worried about? I'm doing great."

"Yeah, but what if somebody finds out you've died and you're a ghost? I mean, suppose they find your body?"

"Are you kidding? I'm at the bottom of the river, and I don't mean the LA River."

"Do you know how weird I would look if any kids at school found out about you? They'd probably start calling me Casper's daughter."

Diane stopped for a light and Elliot glanced at her. For his part she seemed a little dramatic, but the look on her face indicated real concern. He was about to respond when a male voice called, "Yo, Diane! Lemme in, will ya? I need a ride!"

Diane and Elliot looked at the teenage guy standing by the passenger side of the car. To Diane the guy looked like he should be giving concerts. To Elliot he looked like the top nominee for the Maalox Moment-of-the-Year Award.

"What is it?" Elliot asked.

"Daddy, it's Tony Ricker. Do not embarrass me!"

"No, but you're not going to let him in here."

Actually Diane had no choice, and neither did Elliot. Tony Ricker hopped in, squeezing alongside Elliot without seeing him. "Hey, thanks, babe," he told Diane. "You're looking sweet."

"Yeah, thanks, man," Diane replied. "You too."

"I know I am," Tony said with all the modesty he could muster.

The light changed and Diane rolled off, while Elliot rolled his eyes and wondered if he was going to be able to keep his word. Diane seemed enthralled by every word spilling out of the young monster's mouth, and she also seemed intent on pretending Elliot wasn't there.

"I seen your friend Jonelle at the mall, you know," Tony went on, "and I told her how much I dig you, but she goes, you know, like how I should keep dreaming. I couldn't tell if she was putting me down, putting me on, or putting me aside. I told her I'd give you something to dream about. Are you dreaming it?"

"Oh, Tony," Diane whispered, "I didn't even know you liked me."

No, Elliot told himself, *it's your imagination. Ghosts can't gag.*

Brightened by the news, Tony said, "Let's not get carried away here. I'm just saying you turn me on, so I must turn you on. Maybe we should just lock lips for a day or two."

This, Elliot thought, was worse than drowning.

"Cool your jets, pal," Diane said calmly, "or you're off the case."

Once Elliot realized she wasn't talking to him, he was pleased with her response, but Tony wasn't ready to quit. He wiggled his tongue and made some loud kissing sounds. He didn't know it, but he was only inches from Elliot's face and Elliot knew it.

"Oh," Diane said, "I'm going to have to cool my own jets."

With that inspiration Tony moved closer to Diane—and much closer to Elliot. *I can't take this guy,* Elliot thought. He searched Diane's purse for something to get Tony to back off. Finally he found the perfect item—a sharp nail file.

Taking hold of the file, Elliot prepared to jab Tony with it. Tony noticed the file moving through space at about the same time Diane saw it. He froze, and Diane grabbed the file away from Elliot and put it in her purse. "These new lightweight materials are amazing," Diane remarked. "Things just seem to float out of your pocketbook."

"Oh, yeah," Tony said, anxious to show he *knew* about everything. "I had one just like that."

They rode on for a while. "Get him out of here," Elliot whispered.

"No way," Diane replied, "and be quiet!"

"What?" Tony asked.

"I was just wondering if you have to be quiet?"

"Of course not. I was thinking about lightweight materials. These pants are made from them, so don't be surprised if they just float off me."

Tony didn't even get the opportunity to touch his belt. Elliot screamed in his ear and Tony leapt back in fear. Elliot went right after him, beating him on the head and shoulders, while Diane struggled to stop her enraged father.

Determined to be rid of Tony, Elliot reached over him and opened the car door. Next he dumped Tony onto the pavement. From there Tony watched the car drive off and tried to understand how Diane had opened the door and kicked him out. It hadn't seemed as if she was close enough. If he ever rode with her again, he thought, he definitely had to buckle up.

Back in the car, Diane was shaking with rage. Elliot had ruined things with Tony Ricker. "I cannot believe you did that!" she roared.

Still furious about Tony's words and deeds, Elliot shuddered to think about what was going to happen to Diane when he was no longer around. "You are never, ever, *ever* going out with that slime bag!" he announced.

Diane pouted. "Tony Ricker just happens to be one of the few guys who ever noticed me," she said. "I'll see him if I want to! Any time I want to!"

"You'll see him over my dead body!"

"It looks that way," Diane screamed, just before she skidded to a stop.

CHAPTER 17

The screeching brakes caught Stuart and Danny's attention. They were in front of the Hopper house, and Stuart immediately said, "Your sister ought to learn how to stop a car."

"You ought to teach her," Danny said sarcastically. "Oh, I forgot you rode into a bush the other day. Sorry."

Stuart wasn't listening. Diane had climbed out of the car and it seemed as if she were going to cry. "If you've now decided to play daddy," she said, "you can do it for Danny and Amanda. At this point I can handle myself, but thank you very much all the same. I'd like to be able to pursue my pathetic social life without interference."

Diane paused momentarily before going on and continuing her conversation with nobody, as far as Stuart could tell. When she stomped into the house, Stuart looked toward Danny for some sort of explanation.

"Diane's having a nervous breakdown," Danny said, trying hard to sound convincing.

"Is that a good reason for acting crazy?" Stuart asked.

While Danny puzzled over Stuart's question Elliot puzzled over Diane's tears. He followed her into the kitchen. There it was dark enough for Elliot to come into view, and as soon as he did, he said, "Are you through crying, Diane?"

Diane's crying was over, but her anger hadn't subsided. "Go away!" she said, and turned on the light to get him out of sight.

"Oh, that's kind of you," Elliot grumbled, almost to himself. "Trying to reason with the living is just about impossible."

"No," Diane protested, "it's dead people who can be jerks when they want!"

Elliot held his tongue. He felt as if he were going to flicker, and that reminded him of Sir Edith's warning about saving energy. While he watched, Diane checked the answering machine and found there was a message. "I hope this is Tony," she said tauntingly.

"If Tony Ricker shows up around here," Elliot said, disregarding his need to conserve energy, "I'll haunt him to death."

"Hopper," blasted an angry voice from the answering machine, "I don't know where you've been, but I know where you're going if I don't hear from you—immediately!"

The thump of the receiver being slammed down ended the message. Elliot groaned. Mr. Collins's voice was all too familiar to him, but the prospect of keeping him at bay until Thursday was beginning to appear remote.

Elliot's thoughts about Collins were interrupted by Diane slamming drawers in the pantry as she considered what she might cook for dinner. "With all the work I do around here," she said, moaning, "anyone would think I could choose my own friends, but that's not the case. Not here."

"Diane," Amanda said, strolling into the kitchen, "who are you talking to?"

"Who else? Our very own Casper."

Smiling enthusiastically, Amanda turned off the light and said, "Hi, Daddy."

"Hi, sweetie."

Though happy to see Amanda, Elliot's mind was elsewhere. "We'll get to your problems later," he told Diane as he picked up the phone. "Right now I have to deal with my office."

Diane wasn't interested. "All I get is grief around here," she said. "I clean up, I do the laundry, I do everything."

"I take out the garbage," Amanda corrected.

Diane's mind was elsewhere too. She rambled on while Amanda struggled with the garbage pail, which was too big and heavy for her.

Elliot put down the phone. "I cook the meals," Diane said, "and what do I get for it? Nothing but complaints."

"I don't complain about your cooking," Elliot replied.

"Oh, tell me another story."

"Amanda," Elliot said, noticing her struggle, "you're going to hurt yourself."

Elliot lifted the pail and started carrying it out. Amanda reached up and touched the bottom of the pail. She was determined to help. For her part, Diane decided the discussion wasn't over and followed Elliot to the door. "I'll tell you about last Saturday morning," she said. "I'll even use your words: 'Diane, how can you mess up cornflakes?' Does that jog your memory?"

Continuing on his way with the garbage, Elliot walked by the side of the house, not too far from the spot where Danny and Stuart were sitting. "It does nothing for my memory," Elliot called back.

His words caught Stuart's attention, but all he could see was Amanda carrying a gigantic garbage pail with one hand. "Where's your father?" Stuart asked. "I just heard him."

"My father?" Danny said, feigning surprise. "I guess he's at work."

"Diane," Elliot called, "let's face it. This isn't about food."

"Hear that, Danny?"

Danny gave Stuart a wide-eyed stare. "Are you feeling all right?" he asked.

"It's about your being ticked off that I don't want you going out with some real creep," Elliot continued.

Stuart stared at Danny, who was concentrating on keeping a straight face. Something weird was going on with the Hoppers. Stuart was sure of that, and he was equally sure Danny wasn't about to give him even a hint. "Maybe I do feel a little peculiar," he said. "I'm going home."

"Yeah, you should," Danny said. "It could be mumps. They hurt your ears."

While Danny struggled to get rid of Stuart, Diane struggled to get

Elliot off her back. "I'm not your responsibility anymore," she told him as soon as he reentered the kitchen, "so why do you care what I do?"

"Why do I care? I'm surprised you have to ask a question like that."

The doorbell interrupted Elliot. "Amanda, honey," he said, "would you please see who that is and get rid of them?"

"Okay, Daddy," she replied, and rushed off.

"Now, young lady, let me answer your question. I'm your father, and I love you."

Frowning, Diane said, "You don't love me."

"What are you talking about? Of course I love you. You're my daughter."

"Right. I know, and what you feel for me is what fathers feel for daughters. It's not really love. It's father stuff."

"Daddy," Amanda said, interrupting, "it's Joan."

"Joan!" Elliot said, realizing he had forgotten all about her.

"You want to hot-tub with her?"

"Oh, no. Really, no. She can't see me anymore, remember?"

"Oh, yeah," Amanda said, starting for the front door.

"Look," Diane went on, "you only love me because I'm your daughter. You don't love me for who I am. I could have turned out to be anybody, and you'd still feel the same way about me. You didn't even know it was going to be me."

"Right. That's love for you."

"No it's not! Romeo and Juliet is love! He took poison for her. What have you ever done for me?"

"I ate the cornflakes, didn't I?"

Mouthing an incoherent response, Diane promptly walked out of the room.

"Diane!" Elliot anxiously called after her.

CHAPTER 18

"Wasn't that your father's voice?" Joan asked.

"Yes," Amanda admitted, "but he says you can't see him anymore."

If Elliot had heard Joan or Amanda, he might have altered his course, but his every thought was on Diane. He had followed her to her room, but she slammed the door in his face. Instead of walking through it, Elliot knocked. "Diane," he pleaded, "come on out here and talk to me."

In response Diane turned up her stereo. Elliot fought the impulse to step through her door and shut off her stereo. He knocked again and called, "Diane, please stop this!"

Diane raised the volume on her stereo, and Elliot decided to give up. He turned and saw Amanda coming his way.

"Daddy," she said, "I have a message from Joan."

"What is it?"

"Joan says you should try dropping dead."

"Thanks, Amanda. Say, you didn't say I already was dead, did you?"

"No."

"Dad," Danny said, moving down the hallway, "I need to talk

with you. How am I going to be a career magician in school tomorrow without the Trunk of Doom trick?"

"Let me just deal with this Joan thing first, okay?"

"Sure, but—"

The sound of the doorbell cut off Danny's response. "That's probably Joan now," Elliot surmised. "She can't see me in this light. Danny, you go on and let her in and show her to the den. It's nice and dark in there, so I'll be able to go in and talk to her."

"Okay," Danny said, clearly disappointed with his father.

"We'll talk after that, I promise," Elliot said soothingly.

Danny went downstairs, and without telling him, Elliot tagged along. He wanted to get a sense of Joan's mood, but what he got was a sense of Mr. Collins's mood. He, Mr. Seymour, and four other company executives glared in at Danny.

"Hello there, little boy," Mr. Collins said. "Is your daddy home?"

Elliot knew if he were still alive, he would want to die. He was standing right in front of Collins and the others, but they couldn't see him. "Mr. Collins," he called, trying to sound as if he were in another room, "what a nice surprise! I'll be right with you."

Collins and the others stepped past Danny. "Great acoustics in this house," one man whispered. "I would have sworn Hopper was right here."

Collins wasn't interested in acoustics. "Hopper," he called, "your secretary told us you were home. Later on I'll ask you what you're doing home, but right now all these busy people are waiting for you. Let's get moving and close this deal!"

Elliot stuck out his tongue and made several other faces at Collins and his cohorts. Then he threw his voice and called, "Danny, please show our guests to the den. I'll be down in a few minutes."

Following Danny's direction, Mr. Collins and the others moved into the den with no idea they had passed by the ghost of Elliot Hopper along the way. For Elliot the time for face making and joking was over. Before Danny went into the darkened den, Elliot moved alongside him and whispered, "Stall them for as long as you can."

"I'll try," Danny whispered back, but Elliot had already gone off to get into his visible disguise.

Elliot dressed quickly, wearing the same clothes he had worn for his physical. The sight of Collins and the other guys tagging along after him had brought Elliot to an important decision. His boss and the stooges could wait. First he needed to see Joan and do some explaining.

A strong wind greeted Elliot when he stepped outside. He looked in all directions, and as far as he could tell, no one was watching. So he stepped off toward Joan's house.

No one within view was watching, but one person *was* watching. It was Stuart, and he hadn't been the least bit fooled by his friend Danny's efforts to cover up the weird doings at the Hopper house.

Instead of going home, Stuart had hopped on his bike and raced to Stanton's Pro Sports Shop. There he had purchased the best binoculars in stock. After racing home he had just taken up a position on his porch when the "thing" appeared in the Hopper doorway.

Focusing in, Stuart decided the "thing" was definitely Mr. Hopper, but why had he loaded himself down with heavy winter clothing? And why did he have a scarf covering his face?

Unaware of Stuart and unafraid of the wind, Elliot continued on his way. A few seconds later a sharp gust swelled his overcoat like a wind-filled sail and lifted him off the ground. Elliot didn't know if he was imitating a boat or a kite, but as he flapped his arms and legs in an effort to regain control, he realized he was going fast—and in the right direction. Finally he grabbed a tree and stopped himself.

Holding the tree with one hand, Elliot brushed aside his scarf to get a clearer picture of how far he was from the railing leading to Joan's front steps. A few seconds later he hurriedly pulled the scarf back in place. If Joan had been watching from her window, he thought, she might not answer a doorbell sounded by a headless man. Fortunately, he decided, she wasn't the snooping type.

Elliot waited for the wind to ease a little before he rushed to the railing and pulled himself up to Joan's front door. She answered the bell almost immediately and looked aghast at what she guessed was Elliot.

"Please," he said, "I don't have much time, but there's a logical explanation for everything."

"Well, suppose you start by telling me why you're dressed like that."

"Let me come inside. There's too much wind out here."

"Okay, but don't think I'm going to fall for a lot of wind."

Elliot followed her into the living room. "Okay," she said, facing him, "you can take your mask off now. The sheriff and his posse just rode off."

"Not funny," Elliot replied. "And by the way, this room is too bright. Can we go into your bedroom?"

"And I'm a little too bright for that," Joan said angrily. "What's going on with you?"

"I'm begging you. I need to go in there because it's a dark room. I have a sensible explanation, too, but I only have a minute."

Joan stared long and hard at the overdressed sight before her. "All right," she finally announced, "but your story had better be excellent."

CHAPTER 19

Elliot wasted no time, whipping off his scarf and gloves as soon as they entered the darkened room. "Joan, I'm crazy about you," he said. "The times we've spent together have been fantastic, and believe me, I would never say or do anything to hurt you."

"Okay," Joan said, wondering when he was going to get to the point.

"Okay!" he echoed enthusiastically. "I can't tell you how glad I feel about clearing that up. Thanks for your understanding. I have to leave now."

"Just a minute! You can't just leave like that."

"What?" Elliot replied, trying to back away as Joan pulled off his overcoat.

"You need to calm down. You've been overworking. You need to relax."

"Actually," Elliot confessed, "I need to concentrate just to keep myself together."

"Nonsense!" Joan said, attempting to pull him toward her.

Elliot strained to keep her hands from going through him, and in his effort to back out of her reach he fell on the bed and went right through it. When he popped out from under the bed, Joan leapt in fear.

"Wow, Joan," he said, "did you kiss me?"

"How did you get—"

"I'm never going to forget this," Elliot interrupted as he hastily pulled on his overcoat and gathered his other clothing.

Joan sat down on the bed. "It's too dark in here," she said, almost to herself. "You begin seeing things when it's too dark."

"Not another word, Joan. Let's try to remember this as our moment."

Joan watched him leave. If he doesn't need a psychiatrist, she decided, she *most definitely* needed an eye doctor.

Scurrying back to the house, Elliot realized that daylight had given way to evening. "Danny," he said upon entering the front door, "they're still in there, aren't they?"

"Yeah, but I just ran out of magic tricks, and that is something I need to talk to you about."

"You didn't light up the room?"

"No, Dad, everything is pretty cool in there, but I need to talk to you—"

"Listen," Elliot interrupted, "I have to deal with these guys first."

Danny nodded sadly. "Okay," he said.

Elliot tossed off his disguise and quickly gathered some of his paperwork. Then he rushed into the den. "Gentlemen," he said after determining the assembled group could see him, "I've got all the documents here. I was delayed because I had to go through them, but I know we can resolve this whole thing now."

A disbelieving group eyed Elliot with hostility. Recapturing their confidence wasn't going to be easy. Elliot pondered his next move, but the ringing of the phone settled the matter. "Excuse me," he said as he lifted the receiver.

Following Elliot's greeting, the voice on the other end said, "Hello, Mr. Hopper. Stuart calling."

"Oh, yeah. I'll get Danny to pick up—"

"No, it's you I want to speak with," Stuart said. "I know that you're an alien."

"What?"

"I want fifty thousand dollars in small, unmarked bills right away, or I tell the newspapers and TV stations about you. Geraldo will pay a lot for information about an alien."

Elliot stood there, listening to a dial tone. Stuart had hung up on him. If I still had blood, Elliot thought, it would be boiling. "Gentlemen," he said, "I'll be back in a minute."

"Hopper," Mr. Collins said, "just what do you think you're doing?"

"I'm going to be right back."

Enraged, Collins turned to the others, and like trained puppets, they shook their heads in disgust. Had they given Elliot their attention at the moment, they would have seen him leave the room by walking through the door.

While Collins grumbled about Elliot's actions, Stuart Williams stared at his phone, wondering if he had made a mistake. Maybe he should have given Mr. Hopper a chance to respond. Maybe he should call again.

Elliot interrupted Stuart's thoughts with a hard rap on the window. Stuart looked up and blinked in amazement. Mr. Hopper hadn't climbed to the second floor of the Williams house, but he was there, just outside Stuart's window, floating in space. "Listen to me, you little weasel," he said. "If you so much as breathe a word of this to any living thing, I'll do things to you that you can't even imagine."

Stuart seemed frozen in fear. His lips appeared to move, but no words came out of his mouth.

"Don't ever think of threatening me ever again," Elliot continued. "I don't get frightened, I *give* frightened."

"I didn't mean to threaten you," Stuart whispered.

Elliot pulled out a flashlight, and just before shining it on his face he said, "See how you like this one, Stuart."

Elliot's head disappeared and Stuart screamed. "I didn't mean a thing," he cried out.

"Are you going to keep your slimy little trap shut?"

"Yes, I'll never tell anyone," Stuart said, sniveling like a baby. "Just please don't hurt me!"

"There's one more thing you need to know, you whining little creep," Elliot said proudly. "I'm not an alien. I'm a ghost!"

Following that announcement, Elliot flew for home, and Stuart showed his respect for ghosts—by passing out.

Except for Danny, the den appeared to be empty when Elliot returned. "Where are they?" he said anxiously. "Where did they go?"

"They left," Danny said matter-of-factly.

"Left?"

"Left is right," Danny replied. "They were ticked. By the way, I have a little problem of my own. Tomorrow is Career Day at school, and I can't go there and do my old tricks."

Elliot felt overwhelmed. "Danny," he said, "we've all got problems. I'd like to help, but I may have lost my job, and when you consider that comes on top of losing my life, you can understand what I'm getting at."

Danny wasn't sure he fully understood, but he understood enough. The help Elliot had once promised wasn't coming. Danny was going to have to deal with Career Day on his own.

Reaching for the phone, Elliot almost jumped out of his figurative skin when it sounded. He angrily picked it up and said, "Hello."

"Put Diane on," a slightly familiar voice replied. "This is Tony Ricker."

Bells rang in what was passing for Elliot's head. He sneered almost in disbelief. Getting kicked out of the car wasn't enough of a hint for the young man. "Tony Ricker," Elliot said skeptically.

"Yeah, that's me," Tony said.

Putting his hand over the receiver, Elliot told Danny, "This Ricker is another one of my problems. I just hope what I'm about to do works."

Two seconds later the ghost of Elliot disappeared into the phone receiver. "Wow!" Danny said enthusiastically. "Now that is some trick!"

Danny held the receiver to his ear. He could hear Tony Ricker's favorite music blasting away. He put his eye to the receiver. "What are you doing?" Diane asked.

"You wouldn't believe me if I told you," Danny said, "but you have to leave this phone off the hook for Dad."

"What is that supposed to mean?"

"Just trust me and leave it off the hook," Danny replied. "When Dad shows up, he'll explain it to you."

"Where is he?"

"I'm not totally positive, but I think he's at Tony Ricker's house."

"Oh, no!" Diane groaned.

At the same time Tony Ricker also groaned. A hand followed by an arm had sprung from his telephone mouthpiece and grabbed him by the neck.

As Tony struggled to shake loose, the upper body of the man holding his neck also popped out of the mouthpiece. "If you ever call, talk to, wave at, or even think about Diane Hopper again, I will personally tear off your head and attach your neck to a sewer pipe! Is that in plain enough English?"

"Yes." Tony gasped, trying to get some air.

Elliot relaxed his grip slightly. "Are you the devil?" Tony seriously asked.

Elliot shook his head. "I'm worse," he answered, releasing Tony at the same time. "I'm from Pacific Bell."

A terrified Tony watched Elliot disappear into the mouthpiece and heard his voice command: "Now count to five hundred. Then destroy this phone."

"Yes!" Tony screamed into the receiver, and immediately started counting.

CHAPTER 20

Elliot's enthusiastic description of his encounter with Tony Ricker horrified Diane. "How could you do something like that?" she asked.

"Diane, that guy is all bad news. His room is a mess and the posters on his walls are disgusting. Believe me, I'm helping you."

"That's not the kind of help I need. In case you haven't noticed, I've been going through some heavy changes lately. My friends at school are doing all kinds of things, but I'm not doing anything except sticking around this place and raising two kids. The kind of help I really need is a good talk with Mom. She would understand, but she's not here anymore, and neither are you."

"I guess I understand how you feel, but you don't have to be so cranky about it. After all, I'm the one who just died."

"And I'm the one with no life," Diane said, shrugging off his response. "I'm your driver now. I'm their mother. I can't go on like this, and I'm not kidding."

Elliot watched Diane's angry departure. He felt terrible. Some of his proverbial chickens were coming home to roost, and he found himself wishing they had shown up while he was alive. "Hey, what was it you wanted me for?" he called to Danny, who was going upstairs to his room.

"Forget it, Dad," Danny replied. "I don't think you're very good at helping anyone these days."

Saddened by another rejection, Elliot slowly walked into the living room and sat down on the couch. He needed to think. His family seemed to be coming apart. Or had it been coming apart for some time? Had he been too busy to notice?

Upstairs, Amanda clicked on the cassette player, and Elliot's voice soon broke the quiet in the house. His taped version of "The Canterville Ghost" had the attention of everybody, including Elliot.

Amanda enjoyed the tape. Elliot sadly wished he had been around for live performances of Oscar Wilde's ghost tale. Danny gloomily decided to get by in school—by himself. And Diane nostalgically leafed through the family photo album and brushed aside her tears each time she came to a picture of her mom.

As the night went on, Elliot flickered a few times. He tried to tell himself to relax and forget about the flickering, but it worried him. He had a lot to do, and his time was running out.

"I'm sorry to be waking you so early," he told Diane the next morning, "but I have to be at work before everybody else."

"Why don't you fly down there?" Diane said grumpily.

"I need to save the energy I have left," Elliot said. "I really must."

"Okay," Diane said, "I'll drive you and come back here to make sure Danny and Amanda get off all right."

A little later, during the ride to the office, Elliot said, "I'm sorry things are the way they are. If I were living, I'd do things differently."

"I know you would," Diane said sympathetically, but she truly wasn't convinced.

The early-morning traffic was worse than Diane had imagined it would be. After dropping off Elliot she raced home. It was getting late, and she was convinced Danny and Amanda were still fast asleep. She was wrong, but she just managed to get home in time. As she walked into the kitchen she heard the school bus honking. "That's for you," she told Danny.

"No fooling?" Danny said sarcastically as he shakily hoisted up a large trunk and headed for the bus stop.

Surprised by the trunk, and by the words *The Trunk of Doom* crudely lettered on its side, Diane followed him outside and said, "I thought you couldn't do your tricks without the kit Dad forgot to get for you."

"I'll do it without his help," Danny said solemnly.

"Danny, is that safe?"

Danny crossed the street and got on the bus, leaving Diane's question unanswered.

"Oh, Danny," Diane whispered as the bus pulled away, "please be careful."

The image of Danny getting on the school bus with his Trunk of Doom stuck with Diane. Later, when she was walking to class with Jonelle, she decided Danny might need help even if he didn't want it. "Jonelle," she said, pausing by a pay phone, "I have to call my dad."

"Go on," Jonelle said, smiling at the boys passing and greeting her. "We have time."

Just then Diane spotted Tony Ricker coming toward them. "Hi, Tony," she called.

At first Tony squinted to see who was calling him. Then he got a clear picture of Diane, and his eyes almost popped out of his head. A second later he was running in the other direction, knocking students out of his way.

"What stung his butt?" Jonelle asked.

Diane shrugged, but she knew better. "Hi, Carol," she said into the phone, "may I speak with my dad? It's very important."

Carol was in Elliot's office, but she wasn't alone with him. He was making a slide presentation to Mr. Collins and a large assemblage of company executives. "Are you sure it can't wait?" Carol asked.

"I'm positive!"

"All right, Diane, I'll tell him."

"Well," Elliot told the group, "this brings me to capital gains."

"Excuse me, Elliot," Carol interrupted, "but your daughter is on the phone and she says it is very important."

Elliot's immediate reaction was to take the call and find out what was wrong, but the enraged expression on Mr. Collins's face scared him. "I can't talk to her now," he whispered, "but try to find out what's the matter."

Although she was irritated at not being able to get through to Elliot, Diane held her anger in check long enough to provide an abbreviated message about Danny. Then she slammed down the receiver.

"What's bothering you?" Jonelle asked.

"Oh," Diane said, "I just wish Elliot had some time to talk to me. He's always busy."

"Hey, that's nothing to complain about. My dad seems to be around all the time. Sometimes I think he isn't around and he just pops up—like a ghost."

Diane laughed. "It doesn't work that way," she said.

"What are you talking about?"

"Just talking garbage," Diane replied, "but we'd better get to class or we'll be popping up in the office begging for an admit slip."

CHAPTER 21

Danny knew his older sister was worried about him. He was worried too. He'd had a good presentation planned for Career Day, and he had been confident that Mr. Turner, his teacher, and his classmates would be thrilled by The Trunk of Doom kit. Now he had no confidence. He guessed he could do the trick he had thrown together as a replacement, but he didn't think it would be a big hit.

Glancing around the classroom, Danny realized the other kids were totally bored with Stuart's presentation. *I should do better than this*, he thought, turning back toward Stuart, who was at the front of the room.

"Some truly wonderful people have helped to make high finance and leveraged buyouts an exciting field," Stuart said in closing. "And because most of them are now in jail, someone needs to fill the vacuum that exists. Why not me? Thank you."

Danny and two other kids applauded. "Thank you, Stuart," Mr. Turner said, tossing a dirty look at one kid who had booed. "In the future, when any of us hear of vacuums, we'll think of you."

"Maybe we should call him Hoover," one kid called out, and several others laughed.

"Not funny," Mr. Turner remarked. "Let's get to our next presentation. Daniel Hopper."

Danny pulled his trunk to a spot in front of Mr. Turner's desk. "This is going to be a drag," a kid in the third row called out.

"Still not funny," Mr. Turner remarked, but two girls giggled their approval.

Danny faced the class, looking very serious about what he had to say. "As many of you know," he began, "I have long dreamed of a career as a professional magician."

Someone in the back replied with a loud snoring noise, and a ripple of giggles followed it. Danny's determination matched his seriousness. Shrugging off the ridicule, he motioned to the classmates he had asked to assist him, and they hurried to the front of the room.

"In a moment," Danny said, "my assistants are going to blindfold me, wrap chains around me, and lock them in place. While they're working, I'll tell you a little more about the career."

Danny's assistants liked their assignment and immediately set to work on him. "The mean annual income for magicians is under ten thousand dollars," Danny reported.

"You can make more at Burger King," someone called out.

A few students laughed, but Danny continued. "Most magicians are forced to work at conventions and children's parties."

"Maybe you can do my little sister's birthday," a boy in the first row called, "and make her disappear."

"Not funny," Mr. Turner said, and the laughter immediately died down.

"The chains are in place and locked," one assistant told Danny, who was already blindfolded.

"Now help me into the trunk," Danny said.

A hush came over the class as Danny was assisted into the trunk. Standing, he didn't appear small enough to fit inside the trunk when it was closed, and the students wondered if that was what Danny intended.

"I'm going to be doing the Trunk of Doom trick," Danny explained. "Today, because of commercially sold tricks, any moron can perform this trick."

"We can see that," someone called.

"I'm not any moron," Danny shot back. "Anyway, I don't have any commercially sold props, for reasons that are too personal and painful to divulge. Therefore I will have to escape from this trunk using only my magician's skills. No trick props. No easy out."

Danny began to lower his chained body into place. Looking on seriously, Mr. Turner said, "Daniel, are you sure this is safe?"

"To be honest, I'm sure it's not, but there comes a time when a young man must move into action. Every young man has a time when he can't rely on Dad anymore. Then he has to prove to himself that he's a man on his own."

Thinking Danny's speech was part of his routine, a few students applauded. "Well, okay," Mr. Turner said, "go on and do your stuff."

After getting as low as he could, Danny braced himself for the pushing and shoving from his assistants. It was a tight squeeze but Danny fit, and the trunk lid was quickly lowered over him and shut tight.

Danny wasted no time. On his first move he attached the blindfold to a tiny hook inside the trunk. Then he jerked his head and the blindfold came free.

Next Danny opened his mouth and stretched his hand to grab the small key on his tongue. When his hand was inches away from the key, it fell to the floor. Danny twisted quickly and tried to reach the key. There was no room to maneuver. He couldn't get to the key, but he could feel the sweat running down his forehead.

Be calm, he told himself, but his next effort was anything but calm. The trunk shook and rattled, and Danny heard some students laughing. He looked through a small pinhole he had made in the trunk and saw some other students shaking their heads in disgust. "Five dollars says the janitor has to get him out of there," one student called.

The remark got a big laugh, and Danny pulled away from the pinhole, feeling totally humiliated. "Danny," Mr. Turner called, "are you all right?"

"Yeah," Danny answered, but his lack of confidence was apparent.

The boos and groans that followed added to Danny's humiliation, but he refused to give up trying for the key with his mouth. When he had failed again, the frustration became too much for him to take. He banged his head against the walls of the trunk.

Sensing Danny's frustration and concerned for his well-being, Mr. Turner leaned close to the trunk and said, "Danny, what's going on in there?"

The clamor in the classroom immediately died down as each student strained to hear Danny's response. "Mr. Turner," Danny said.

"Yes, Danny."

"Could you please call the janitor to help me?"

To Danny the roar of student laughter was almost unbearable. He couldn't remember a time when he had felt so ashamed. "Stuart," Mr. Turner called over the noise, "run downstairs and get the janitor."

Danny hoped Stuart went fast. He wanted out of the trunk—and out of school, for that matter. As soon as the janitor freed him, he was leaving. He had a new career he wanted to try—being a runaway.

CHAPTER 22

Moments later Danny felt as if the trunk were moving. Looking through his peephole, he saw some classmates gaping in amazement at the trunk, which seemed to be rising from the floor. Danny's eyes brightened as a wonderful idea passed through his mind.

"Hiya, Danny boy," Elliot said, pushing his head through the floor of the trunk.

"Dad!" Danny said excitedly. "I just knew it was you."

"Yeah," Elliot said, struggling to lift the trunk higher, "but you've gained weight."

"The janitor is busy!" Stuart called out.

Danny immediately looked through the peephole and spotted Stuart by the classroom door. His eyes opened wide at the sight of the rising trunk. Then they rolled back and he slumped to the floor. He had fainted again.

"Your friend really needs to work on his self-control," Elliot said with a grunt.

"Hey," Danny said, "I thought you had a big meeting today."

"I did, but your sister left a message telling me she was worried about you and this trick. I got worried, too, and I decided you were a lot more important than the boring meeting. So here I am."

Danny beamed with pride as Elliot used his teeth to loosen some of his bindings. Once they were loose enough, Danny got the key and unlocked the chains. "Thanks, Dad," Danny said. "You don't know how much this means to me."

"You're welcome, son. Now let's give them a classy finish—one they'll never forget."

Danny moved into position while Elliot slowly lowered the trunk onto Mr. Turner's desk. Once it was in place, Danny opened the lid. Then, with Elliot doing the lifting, Danny floated straight up over the trunk.

Several girls screamed, and several boys scrambled for cover behind some other girls. Looking down at Mr. Turner, Danny said, "How am I doing?"

"You just pulled an *A* out of my hat," Mr. Turner remarked.

"Corny," Elliot whispered to Danny as he closed the trunk and lowered his son into a sitting position on it.

Danny smiled, and his classmates greeted him with a standing ovation. "Dad," Danny said, his whisper almost drowned out by the applause, "you're the greatest."

"Thanks, Danny. I'll see you later."

Elliot literally flew back to his office, but as he suspected, it was no longer filled with company executives. They'd been dismissed, but Mr. Collins was waiting, along with Mr. Seymour and Mr. Nero. "I'm terribly sorry I had to leave," Elliot began, trying hard to think of a lie Mr. Collins could live with.

"You're terribly sorry," Mr. Collins said mockingly. "You are definitely a worthless piece of slime."

"I wouldn't go that far," Elliot mumbled.

"He's a little upset," Mr. Seymour explained.

"Really?" Elliot replied.

"I can't believe you would walk away," Mr. Collins said, "just at the very time we were closing negotiations."

"I didn't walk," Elliot half whispered.

"I'm sure Hopper had an excellent reason for walking off," Mr. Seymour said, looking for Elliot to pick up on his comment.

"If I hadn't stepped in," Collins went on, "the deal would have fallen through, and I'd have had to kill you."

"Too late," Elliot mumbled, and bit his lip to keep from smiling.

"Well," Seymour said, turning his attention to Elliot, "we closed the deal, so he doesn't really have to kill you now."

"That's absolutely right," Collins added. "All I have to do now is *ruin* you."

"This is the part where Mr. Collins and I are in total agreement," Seymour said cheerfully.

"You're fired, Hopper!" Collins screamed.

Though Elliot halfway expected he was going to be fired, the actual words upset him. "Mr. Collins," he pleaded, "please give me a chance to—"

"I said, you're fired! That's it! You're fired!"

"You walked out on the meeting," Seymour added.

"I've got a really excellent explanation about that," Elliot answered.

"Fired!" Collins roared. "Fired! Fired!"

"It's not for me," Elliot said quickly, "it's for my kids. Their whole future depends on this. I just can't possibly lose my job right now. I've given everything I have to this company for the past fourteen years. I've served you well and loyally, and I think that has to count for something. It should mean something to you."

Mr. Collins stopped and signaled Seymour to be quiet. Elliot's words had touched the man. He considered them carefully, giving Elliot the benefit of his fourteen years. Then he said, "Hopper, you're fired!"

Feeling lost, and flickering on top of that, Elliot staggered out of his office into Carol's well-lit area. "Don't bother calling Diane for me," he said sadly. "I'm going to walk home."

"Walk home?" Carol said, looking up. "You can't walk that far."

"Too bad," Elliot said. "I already started."

Carol started to voice her disagreement, but she couldn't see Elliot. He certainly had already started. "Take your time," she said, wondering who she was talking to.

On his way Elliot considered everything that had happened since his death. It had served to remind him how little attention he had been giving to his kids. He recalled the look on Danny's face when he'd pushed his head through the bottom of the trunk. Sure, he'd been happy, but he had also looked as if he couldn't believe his father would show up at an important moment. Elliot felt bad about that. In fact, he felt bad about everything.

When Elliot flickered again, he realized he was burning up a lot of his remaining energy with self-pity. So he walked on, trying to think of a way to keep his family together—without him.

Passing his bank and seeing a few people lined up outside by the automatic teller window, Elliot realized he could do a lot more magic than the trick he'd done with Danny. He could pass through the bank's locked doors and then walk right into its safe. He could get all the money his family would need to stay together. But he couldn't tell his kids where he got it because they wouldn't take it. Even worse than that, he realized he couldn't take the money. He didn't even like the things he had done to pass his physical, but now it appeared that didn't make any difference.

It was dark by the time Elliot reached his front door. He paused there, wondering how Diane and the others would take the news. "Elliot," Joan called, "you're not even dressed yet!"

Seeing Joan standing in her doorway in a formal gown, Elliot remembered the banquet they were scheduled to attend. She looked beautiful. "I'm sorry, Joan," he said sadly, "but I just can't talk to you about anything right now."

Elliot's response seemed outrageous to Joan. To control her anger she closed her eyes and counted to ten. When she opened them, Elliot was gone.

CHAPTER 23

As soon as Elliot stepped through the front door he felt himself flicker. This time the sensation was far more severe than any of the previous ones, and it frightened him. "Not yet," he said, but he doubted anyone was listening.

The house was quiet. Elliot stepped into the living room and found the kids sitting there—almost in the dark.

"Hi, Dad," Amanda said immediately.

"Hi," Elliot said, "were you all waiting for me?"

"Not really," Diane answered. "We were listening to Danny's story about how our ghost dad saved the day for him. Now the kids at school think of Danny as Houdini rather than the weirdo who locked himself in a trunk."

"That's great, but I'm afraid I have some bad news for all of you."

"Let me guess," Diane said sarcastically. "You were fired!"

"Yeah, you got it. I guess you could say I blew it, gang. I'm sorry, truly sorry."

"Wonderful news," Diane said. "All week long we have to hear your story about 'wait until Thursday and everything will be super.' Well, let me add to the bad news—Thursday is just about here."

"I said I'm sorry."

"Your going-away present is to tell us you're sorry?" Diane said angrily.

"I'm not sorry," Danny said, interrupting. "I don't care about your job, Dad. When you were alive, you never would have left any meeting to come to help me."

Elliot appreciated Danny's warm smile. "Thanks," he said.

Danny was about to add a few more enthusiastic words when the front door flew open. All eyes focused on Joan, who walked right into the house and said, "Elliot, I don't know what's going on with you, but we've got to have this out right now."

In response Elliot flickered.

"Go ahead. You've always got time for her," Diane whispered, and then abruptly set out for her room.

By then Joan was moving toward Elliot, and Elliot was retreating to a darker part of the room. "Why is it always so dark around here lately?" she asked. "Do you have something to hide?"

Joan's final question sent a chill up Elliot's spine. He was tired of the entire charade. It had gotten him nowhere. "Joan," he said, looking her in the eye, "I'm dead."

"Hey, I'm tired too," she answered. "I work hard all day, but that doesn't give me the right to break dates."

"You don't get it. I'm *really* dead. I'm a ghost."

"That's perfectly normal," Amanda chimed in.

"Watch this," Elliot said, just before turning on a nearby light.

Joan screamed so soon after Elliot disappeared that the entire thing seemed like a simultaneous event. A second later he flipped the light off and immediately reappeared.

In response to Joan's seemingly uncomprehending stare, Elliot shrugged and said, "Dead—as a doornail."

"You're going to have to explain all of this to me," Joan said, fighting off a natural inclination to run right out of the house.

After warning that his story would be hard to believe, Elliot launched into it. When he reached the part about coming out of the river and not being seen by the policeman, he said, "About then I was beginning to think I was dead."

"Actually," a voice said from the doorway, "I'm afraid you're not dead."

Elliot thought he recognized the voice, and the body standing in the doorway matched. It was Sir Edith. "What are you doing here?" Elliot blurted out.

"We'll get to that in good time. Is the kitchen this way? I am famished."

Moving quickly, Elliot blocked Sir Edith's path. "Your trip to the kitchen can wait," he said. "For now you can tell me what you mean about my not being dead."

Joan glanced at Danny and Amanda. Like her, they obviously had no idea who the strange man was or how he had happened to appear there.

"Well, you're not being very hospitable," Sir Edith remarked, "but I'll tell you. I did some calculations on your measurements. You do recall my taking your measurements, don't you?"

"Yes, yes," Elliot said impatiently.

"Well," Sir Edith went on, "you're not a ghost. You're a spirit, all right, but you're definitely not a ghost. Not yet, at least."

Joan didn't know what was going on, but she couldn't just stand by any longer. "Just who is this guy?" she blurted out.

"Oh, I'm terribly sorry for being so rude," Sir Edith said, handing her one of his cards.

"Is that your name?" Joan asked.

"Excuse me," Elliot interrupted, "but can we get back to the matter of me? I'm beginning to lose my spirit."

"Corny!" Danny groaned.

"No one asked you," Elliot replied.

"Well, to put it bluntly," Sir Edith announced, "you didn't die. You just took the occasion to jump out of your body."

"Why would I do something like that?"

"I would say something scared you. Something quite dangerous happened, and it scared you."

"Yeah," Elliot said, thinking about the event he had been describing to Joan, "the taxi went off the bridge and into the river. As a result, I drowned. That's pretty scary."

"Ah, there's where you're wrong. You didn't drown. You merely jumped out of your body."

"Merely?" Elliot repeated. "How often does this happen?"

"Excuse my unfortunate use of *merely*. It doesn't fit your situation. Actually, it's been rumored there was one other case like yours in America. It was years ago. Before the poor chap was able to find his body, he had to wear a bunny costume. The poor fellow wore it for a week."

"A bunny costume?" Elliot said, clearly interested in the details of Sir Edith's story. "Did his name happen to be Arthur Hopper?"

Elliot's question intrigued Sir Edith. "I really don't know," he replied.

"That was my father!" Elliot proudly announced. "I know all about him wearing that bunny suit, but he told us the zipper got stuck."

"Aha, just as I suspected after the measurements. Your ability to jump out of your body is hereditary."

"Wow!" Danny said cheerfully. "This is far-out! How long will it be before I'm able to do it?"

"Just wait your turn, young man," Sir Edith admonished. "Right now your father has a body out in the world somewhere, and we really should try to find it before it checks out for good."

"How?" Joan asked.

"Call in all the body snatchers," Elliot joked, "and grill them until one of them talks."

Danny laughed, but Sir Edith said, "This is not a laughing matter. Elliot could be gone before he can utter another one of his attempts at humor. And if he goes, he's not coming back."

CHAPTER 24

"Okay," Elliot said, winking at Danny, "no more joking. A body like mine deserves to be found. I'll call all the police stations."

"I'm going over to my house and call all the cab companies," Joan announced. "Someone may know something."

On his first call Elliot reached a Sergeant Edith Berger. "Let me talk to him," Sir Edith immediately requested.

"It's a she," Elliot said, holding his hand over the receiver while Danny giggled loudly.

"This is not the time for laughing," Sir Edith told Danny.

"Sergeant," Elliot went on, "did you know about the accident on the bridge on Monday?"

"Tell me a little more about it, please?"

"A cab went into the river."

"Oh, really? Was anybody killed?"

"That's what I want to know. Can you help me?"

"I'm afraid not. This is the first I've heard of the accident. You're going to have to call another precinct."

"Any suggestions?"

"Yes, you're going to have to call another precinct."

Elliot slammed down the phone, trying to recall if he'd given the woman his name. "She sounded as if she might be related to you," he told Sir Edith.

"Really?"

"No," Elliot replied, "but I can tell this isn't going to be easy. I hope Joan gets lucky."

At that moment Joan thought she was lucky. The Allover Alert Cab Company had just answered its phone after thirty-seven rings. "Yeah," a gruff male voice said.

"I'm calling about the cab that fell into the river on Monday."

"Wouldn't you rather ride in a dry cab?" the gruff voice asked.

"No, I don't want *that* cab. I want to find out about the driver and his passenger."

"Lady, it wasn't our cab, but if it was our cab, I wouldn't tell you a thing about it. Do you realize you're using up time on a very busy phone?"

"No, but I do realize I am talking to a moron."

Joan slammed down the phone. She wanted Elliot to live. She glanced through her window toward the Hopper house. She imagined Elliot was hard at work and decided she wasn't going to let one bad call slow her down. Elliot deserved a substantial effort.

"This is a substantial effort," Sir Edith said, unknowingly taking the words out of Joan's head.

"How can you eat so much at a time like this?" Elliott asked.

"I told you I was famished. Say, I'm not kidding about this meat loaf. Your daughter is quite a cook. These things must be pieces of olives she cooked into the loaf."

"They're worms," Danny joked.

"Yeah," Amanda added, "Diane always puts them in for company to enjoy."

Sir Edith almost gagged. "Lovely children you have," he remarked.

"I don't have time for joking," Elliot replied, winking once more at Danny.

"You certainly don't," Sir Edith agreed, just as Elliot flickered again.

With deadly seriousness Elliot began working his way through the telephone book listing of police stations. After a few more unproductive calls, he switched his approach. Instead of asking about the accident he asked if there was any information about Elliot Hopper. Pretending to be a friend, he reported that Hopper had been missing since Monday morning and had last been seen in a cab.

As Elliot failed to learn a thing in call after call, a feeling of gloom fell over the group assembled in the living room. Sir Edith stopped eating, and Danny and Amanda sat there with impassive expressions masking their worst fears. Finally he made his last call and recited his story about Elliot Hopper.

"Okay," Elliot said a few seconds later, "thanks for checking."

"Nothing?" Sir Edith said as Elliot put down the receiver.

"It seems as if Elliot Hopper has disappeared from the face of the earth."

Catching Elliot's remark as she entered the house, Joan said, "It certainly does. The cab companies were no help at all, and you're not at Central Hospital, either. They do have a cabdriver there, and he was brought in on Monday."

"What's his name?" Elliot asked.

"They wouldn't release that information," Joan explained, "and they wouldn't say where he had the accident, but they did say he was an accident victim."

"You must talk to him," Sir Edith told Elliot.

"That's out of the question," Joan said. "They're not even letting close relatives see the man. He's been in a coma since they brought him in, but he's alive. So I guess you could say that somebody up there likes him."

"If you're talking about heaven," Elliot quipped, "somebody up there obviously doesn't know him."

"Dad," Danny said, revealing his fear, "you have to concentrate on finding your body."

Along with the others, Elliot silently considered the situation. Trying to see the cabdriver didn't strike him as particularly useful. The man was in a coma, but even if he was awake and alert, he probably wouldn't make a lot of sense. He hadn't when Elliot was in his cab. He was the reason Elliot had drowned.

Suddenly it hit Elliot. "I didn't drown," he called out. "Look, I'm still here."

"Is your mind going?" Sir Edith asked.

"No, I just mean that I'm not underwater. If the cabdriver survived and nobody found me, that means I'm somewhere else. I must have washed ashore somewhere."

"You must have washed ashore somewhere near the accident," Joan said excitedly. "We can search the riverbank."

"Let's get moving," Elliot said. "Danny, Amanda, call your sister!"

Danny and Amanda raced to the bottom of the stairs. "Diane," Amanda called, "Daddy wants you."

"Hurry up," Danny added. "We have to go to the river and look for Dad's body."

"I'll be right there," Diane called, and jumped off her bed.

She had been in her room for a few hours, missing the arrival of Sir Edith. Danny had run up earlier and told her about the Englishman and the good news he'd brought about Elliot not being dead. Unfortunately Danny had added all the stuff about the missing body and about Elliot going for good if it couldn't be found.

The entire matter depressed Diane. Instead of wanting to listen to every phone call Elliot made, she had opted to stay in her room and hope for the best. Now it sounded as if the best had been accomplished.

After checking herself out in the mirror, Diane raced down the hall. She heard voices downstairs. Then she heard the sound of the front door opening. She picked up her pace and headed down the stairs. On the second step her foot slapped down on a roller skate. She hadn't noticed the skate, and it sent her sailing right through the banister.

The crashing noise caught the attention of Elliot and the others. They turned quickly and rushed back into the house. On the landing below the stairs, they saw Diane's lifeless body. "Oh, no!" Elliot screamed.

CHAPTER 25

Using some first-aid techniques, Joan worked vigorously to revive Diane. After several minutes she said dejectedly, "It's no use. The paramedics may be able to help her, but my guess is she's going to the hospital."

"I'll call 911 right now," Elliot said.

"Say," Sir Edith said, "why don't you allow me to call. You should be on your way to that riverbed. You need to find your body."

"Forget that," Elliot said stubbornly. "Until I know that Diane is all right, I'm not going anywhere."

"I can take care—" Joan started to say.

"I'm sure you can, Joan, but I'm still not going. The riverbed can wait, and so can everything else."

"Is Diane going to be fine?" Amanda asked, tears forming in the corners of her eyes.

"Yes, she is, honey," Sir Edith said assuredly.

Danny wrapped his arm around his younger sister and gently led her toward the living room while Elliot phoned for emergency assistance.

In a few minutes a fire engine and an ambulance arrived at the house. Two firemen entered first, followed by two paramedics. As soon as Elliot ascertained that they could see him, he briefed them on Diane's fall.

After checking Diane's pulse one fireman said, "I'm going to give her a shot of oxygen. Maybe it'll bring her around."

Elliot and the others watched and prayed while the firemen worked over Diane. They obviously knew what they were doing, but Diane didn't respond to any of their efforts. Finally one fireman told the paramedics, "Get your gurney in here. This girl is going to the hospital."

"That's all right with you, isn't it, sir?" the other fireman asked Elliot.

Flickering slightly, Elliot noticed the look of surprise on the fireman's face. "That's fine with me," Elliot said. "I'm just a little nervous."

"I can see that, but don't worry, sir. There are outstanding people working emergency down at Central. Just be calm."

"Thanks," Elliot said, catching Sir Edith's signal that they needed to talk.

When the paramedics returned with the gurney, Elliot slipped off to the side. "You should be looking for your body," Sir Edith again warned. "These people will take good care of your daughter."

"I'm going with Diane."

"What can you do for her?"

Without responding, Elliot went to the side of the gurney and watched as the paramedics strapped Diane into it. He realized he had no logical answer to Sir Edith's question, but he truly didn't think he needed one. Diane needed someone by her side—someone who loved her and wanted only the best for her. Elliot figured that was what he could do for her—even if he was only a spirit. Her ghost dad was sticking around.

"You take the kids and Sir Edith in my car," Elliot told Joan. "I'm going in the ambulance."

"I'll be right behind you," Joan said, taking the car keys from him.

While it didn't seem as if Diane should be in serious condition because of her fall, her failure to regain consciousness concerned the paramedics, and they worked rapidly to get her on the road to the hospital.

Elliot followed them out of the house, and Joan led the kids and Sir Edith to the car. A small crowd had gathered outside, and one person in it was Stuart. He grabbed for Danny's arm and said, "What's happening?"

"Diane fell," Danny said. "They're taking her to the hospital."

"Is she going to be all right?"

"I don't know," Danny said, hurrying to join the others.

As Danny rushed off, Stuart turned and spotted Elliot Hopper in the back of the ambulance. A shiver ran up his spine. He wondered how the paramedics would feel if they knew one of their riders was a ghost. "You don't scare me, Mr. Hopper," he said under his breath, and then looked around to see if he'd been heard.

A minute later the ambulance pulled away, and the crowd of onlookers dispersed, leaving Stuart alone under the streetlight. "Okay, Mr. Ghost," he said fearlessly, "you get your ride to the hospital and see who is there to greet you."

Stuart raced off to his house, glancing over his shoulder at the Hopper house as he ran. His big mouth had gotten him in trouble the last time, he decided, so this time he was going to act anonymously. He had learned what he needed to know about dealing with ghosts.

By the time Stuart reached his room, his newly found courage was fading. Sure, he had seen Mr. Hopper ride off in the ambulance, but there was no telling when he would pop up. Deciding to proceed with caution, Stuart dimmed the lights in his room. Then he sat down by the phone and tried to think of the name of the organization he'd heard about. They would take care of Mr. Hopper. Finally he picked up the receiver and tapped out the numbers for information. "I'd like the number of Ghost Dusters," Stuart said. "I don't know the address."

"One moment please," the operator said.

Stuart got ready to write down the recorded number he expected to hear next. Instead he heard a tapping on his window. "Oh, no," he said, and his body started to shake.

"The information you have requested is not available," the

recorded voice of an operator announced as the tapping on the window repeated.

Stuart needed two hands to put down the receiver. Then he stepped over to the window. If it was who he thought it was, there was no sense in running.

A familiar face smiled through the window at Stuart. It was Diane, and she seemed to be hanging on the window ledge. He quickly opened the window and said, "How did you get up here? I thought you were in the ambulance."

"I jumped out of the ambulance," Diane lied as she threw her legs over the windowsill and stepped into Stuart's room. "Then I climbed the vines to your room. I need your help."

"Did you just find out that your old man is a ghost?" Stuart asked.

"Yeah," Diane said, "and I found out something else too."

"I'm glad you decided to tell me," Stuart said, looking slightly puzzled, "but are you sure you climbed vines to get to my window? I don't remember seeing any vines out there."

"They may have just sprung up," Diane said. "Turn a light on and I'll show you the other thing I found."

"Oh, sure," Stuart said, reaching for the light switch.

As soon as the lights came on, Diane disappeared. Stuart blinked several times, not wanting to believe what had happened. "My father and I don't like rats," Diane said, just before Stuart fainted.

Diane smiled. She was glad she had heard Stuart shooting off his mouth after the ambulance pulled away. She didn't imagine he would be making any more phone calls when he awakened. She still had a lot to do before checking in at the hospital, but being able to fly cut down on the time being used. She concentrated, and within a matter of seconds she was on her way to Jonelle's house.

CHAPTER 26

Jonelle was parking her car when Diane caught up with her. She opened the car door and sat down alongside her friend. "Hi," Jonelle said, looking surprised, "where'd you come from—the sky?"

"Something like that," Diane said. "Just don't jump out of the car. I have a long story to tell you, and not much time to tell it in."

"I don't jump," Jonelle said firmly.

When Diane had finished her story and reinforced part of it with a flashlight from Jonelle's glove compartment, she was delighted by Jonelle's wicked smile. "What are you thinking?" she asked.

"I was thinking of what I would do if I was a ghost," Jonelle remarked. "You can have a lot of fun."

"I can't believe it," Diane said, feigning disgust. "You're supposed to be my best friend, and I tell you that I might be dead, and you don't even act upset."

"Well," Jonelle said, shrugging, "I probably will be upset one of these days, but you seemed in a good mood, and I didn't want you to be unhappy. What are you going to do now?"

"Break the news to Elliot," Diane said. "I don't even know why he had to go to the hospital. Don't you think the firemen or paramedics would have known I was dead?"

"Maybe you get to be a ghost for a little while before you die,"

Jonelle surmised. "Like in the movies, it's a preview of coming attractions."

Diane laughed. "I'm going," she said.

"Drop around anytime," Jonelle said, looking somewhat emotionally distraught, "and take care of yourself."

Concentrating again, Diane reached the hospital in a matter of seconds. There she saw a medical team working feverishly on her lifeless body. She also spotted Joan, Danny, Amanda, and the Englishman who had brought Elliot the good-news bad-news message. They were outside the emergency room, looking tired and sad.

Back inside the well-lit emergency room, Diane observed another invisible form wearing a grim expression. It was Elliot. Floating over to his side, Diane said, "Hey, Dude, cheer up!"

Elliot appeared puzzled and weak. "Diane," he said, "what are you doing?"

"Taking after my old man, I guess."

For a supporting gesture, Diane poked her head through the wall. "Stop fooling around and get back in your body," her father said.

"Not now," Diane said, disappearing through the wall.

Elliot followed and chased her down the hall. When he got close, he called, "Diane, please talk to me?"

"Okay," Diane said, moving close to him.

"How'd you get out of your body?"

"I don't know. I remember falling, and then I was in the closet. When I came out, you were leaning over my body, so I went back in the closet. I came out again when I was being taken to the ambulance."

"You must have been frightened and jumped out of your body," Elliot said. "I gather it's hereditary. Anyway, you have to get back in your body before something serious happens."

"You mean something really serious?" Diane said, suddenly recalling some of her frustrations. "Like having your dad away all the time and then your momma dies? Serious like being a teenager and not being able to have any fun because you've got to raise two kids because your father is too busy? Serious like my not getting any dates like other girls my age? Or serious like having my father die without leaving us any way to take care of ourselves?"

"Diane," Elliot pleaded, "this isn't the time to do this to me."

"It's always about you, isn't it? How this affects you. Unfortunately I'm thinking about me right now, and this being a ghost feels a lot better than the crummy life I've been living. And I'm definitely not going back to it."

"Diane, life is all there is. Believe me."

The cynical grin on Diane's face changed as soon as Elliot flickered. "What was that?" she asked.

"Don't throw your life away," Elliot said, disregarding her question. "I'm begging you. Your life is everything."

Elliot immediately flickered again, but for a longer time. Frightened by what seemed to be happening, Diane said, "Elliot, are you all right?"

"When you're young, you think nothing can happen to you," Elliot said, clearly losing his image and voice as his spirit body continued to flicker. "I never had a care. I put everything off. I kept delaying my happiness—the happiness of our family."

"Elliot!" Diane screamed as he flickered violently and dropped to the floor. "What's happening?"

"Listen to me, Diane, there is no Thursday. The whole thing is about what's here and now. It's about today and tomorrow. Don't do what I did. Don't throw it away."

Diane fought off the tears. "Shouldn't we try to find your body?" she asked.

"That's not important. It's you."

Diane reached down and tried to help him up. "Come on," she said, "I'll help you look."

"No, I'm not doing a thing until you get back into your body."

Feeling just on the edge, Diane said, "Why don't you let me help you?"

"Because I want you to live," Elliot said, struggling with the words as his condition worsened. "I'm your father, and I want you to know what your mother knew. I want you to know what it's like to fall in love. I want you to know what it's like to hold a child in your arms like your momma held you when you were born. Because . . ."

"Because you love me," Diane said knowingly, and the tears ran from her eyes.

Elliot tried to speak, but he had lost most of his remaining energy. Finally he smiled and nodded weakly.

For Diane, the fun of playing ghost was all gone. Elliot was slipping away right before her eyes, and there didn't seem to be a thing she could do about it. "Someone help me," she called in frustration. "Please help me."

Diane immediately realized that no one heard her plea for help. She hadn't been concentrating. Looking around, she noticed they were in the corridor next to the hospital's intensive-care unit.

Without a moment's hesitation Diane rushed into the darkened room. The beds in the room seemed to be filled, and the patients seemed almost lifeless. As Diane's eyes jumped from one bed to another she noticed that each of the patients was hooked to a monitor that kept track of heartbeat and other vital signs.

Suddenly her eyes locked on one bandaged patient. She moved closer to him. "Oh, my God," she gasped, steadying herself to keep from falling on the patient. "I can't believe it!"

CHAPTER 27

Diane flew through the wall of the intensive-care unit. "Come on, Daddy," she said, dragging Elliot through the same wall and into the room.

"What is it?" Elliot asked as Diane pointed him toward a bandaged patient in a nearby bed.

"It's you!" Diane said, releasing Elliot and picking up the patient's chart. "But they have you listed as Curtis Burch."

Elliot gathered up all of his remaining energy and thought hard. "The cabdriver," he said excitedly. "That was his name. I didn't have any ID on me. That crazy Curtis Burch had my wallet."

Diane helped Elliot into a position alongside the bed. "If you get back in your body," she said, "I'll get back in mine."

Elliot nodded, and though he felt very weak, he managed to climb onto the bed and swing himself over his lifeless body. A second later he disappeared into the body, which shuddered slightly before jerking upright. "Wow!" Elliot said, displaying new strength in his voice. "This is really interesting. Hello, Diane."

Coming to his side, Diane said, "Are you all right?"

"I hurt all over, and I feel as if I weigh ten tons."

"You look terrible," Diane said, but her beaming face revealed her happiness.

Elliot alternated between winces and grins. "I can't believe that something that feels so terrible feels so great," he said. "You should try it sometime—like now."

Diane agreed wholeheartedly. She gave Elliot a quick kiss and flew out of the room, hoping her body was still in the emergency room.

The medical team that had started working on Diane when she arrived at the hospital was still working on her. As she flew into the room she heard the lead doctor rattle off a series of orders. He sounded anxious, and the beeping sounds coming from the monitor, along with the wavy lines displayed on it, made Diane outright nervous. "Hang on," she called.

Moving like a track star, Diane hurled herself onto the body being examined and sank into it. As soon as her spirit form disappeared, her human form leapt upright. The nurses jumped away, looking in total amazement at Diane.

"Kowabonga!" she said. "That hurts as much as Elliot said it would, but I'm okay. I really am."

The doctors and nurses looked on as Diane struggled to regain her sense of balance. They were almost convinced they were observing a miracle. "Awesome!" one nurse finally remarked.

"Yeah," Diane agreed, and leapt from the examining table. "Hey, thanks, everybody. I'm okay, and thanks for your help."

Diane walked to the door, but the walk became a sprint as soon as she reached the corridor. "Dad?" she called, seeing a figure in a hospital gown sprinting toward her from the other end.

"Diane?" the figure replied.

They continued toward each other, and once they met, they hugged and whirled each other around joyously. "Oh, Daddy," Diane said, "I can't tell you how glad I am that you're alive."

"Me too," Elliot said. "I mean . . ."

Their eyes met, and they hugged again. There was no need for Elliot to explain. They were happy for each other. They loved each other. "Let's get the others and go home," Diane suggested.

"A splendid idea," Elliot agreed.

Before they could act on the idea, they saw Joan with Amanda in her arms, Danny, and Sir Edith rushing toward them. "Are you both for real?" Joan said cheerfully.

"As real as can be," Elliot replied, "and from now on we're staying in these bodies."

"Right," Diane agreed. "Once a ghost is enough."

"Am I going to jump out of my body someday?" Danny said.

"Young man," Sir Edith said, "your mouth should be washed with soap for even thinking such a thought."

"How old were you when your sense of humor jumped out of your body?" Danny replied.

"Danny," Elliot said, holding back a smile, "you mind your mouth. If it weren't for Sir Edith, I might not be here."

"And if we don't get out of here soon," Joan said, gesturing toward a mob of doctors, nurses, and other hospital personnel gathering in the corridor, "we may never get another opportunity."

Led by Elliot, Diane and the others moved triumphantly through the corridor and the emergency room. Still awed by Elliot's and Diane's miraculous recovery, the doctors and nurses followed them outside.

"Mr. Hopper," a female voice called, "I must speak with you."

Elliot shook off his impulse to keep going. It wasn't polite. "Yes," he said, turning abruptly.

A woman walked up to him and extended her hand. "I'm Marcie Nelson," she said, "from the hospital's public-relations office. I'm here about the amazing recovery of you and your daughter that just took place. It was eyewitnessed by members of our medical staff, and, really, the recovery should be researched and documented. It is absolutely essential that we talk with you. So would you please come with—"

"Not now," Elliot interrupted. "Sorry, but it'll have to be after. I mean, after we've had a chance to spend some time together."

Diane smiled at Joan. "How about after the wedding?" she said.

"Wedding?" Marcie Nelson said as Elliot and Joan traded romantic glances.

Amanda smiled and pointed at her daddy and Joan.

"When is the wedding?"

"When everything is perfectly normal," Amanda said.

"I don't think they should be forced to wait that long," Diane joked.

"Right!" Elliot and Joan agreed.

Then they marched off to the car, leaving Marcie Nelson totally bewildered.

It was late when the car rolled back into their neighborhood. They'd had a joyous ride, listening to Elliot and Diane detail some of the things that had happened to them while they were ghosts. Some parts even amused Sir Edith, and it was beginning to look as if he were going to be around for a while.

Danny was the first to notice the lights in Stuart's room, but as they all looked toward his house, the beam coming from the newly placed spotlight above his window was unmistakable. "I would imagine that's the best spotlight money can buy," Elliot said.

"It'll keep ghosts away," Diane remarked.

"I'll tell him tomorrow," Danny said.

"No, after," Amanda chimed in.

"The wedding?" Danny said, smiling.

"Right!" they all answered.